"But you *it."*

"Yes." The wo... ...se. "I am."

"Then that's all that matters.

For once Willow didn't point out that fun wasn't all that mattered. That responsibility and focus were the keys to stability, and stability the key to happiness. Because today she wasn't sensible Willow Jones, dutiful and perennially worried daughter, sister and aunt, nor was she Willow Jones, high-flying regional finance director, Europe.

Today, for one day only, she was allowing herself to explore the Willow she might have been if she hadn't been forced to grow up so soon. A Willow as carefree and impulsive as any of her family.

She closed her eyes and let Logan pull her close, swaying to the music, her body pressed enticingly close to his. She could feel the hardness of his thigh against hers, the muscles of his taut stomach and broad chest, the strength in his arms. She made herself relax, luxuriating in every inch of contact, her greedy body aching for more. In a day of wild adventures, his company was the wildest thing of all.

Dear Reader,

Marriage of convenience has always been my favourite trope, and so it was a joy to watch Logan and Willow negotiate their way from moment of passion to fulfilling a contract to falling in love. Willow is a woman with a life plan, and that plan does not include a whirlwind Vegas marriage to playboy heir Logan. And yet, when a near accident makes her reevaluate her life, she finds herself responding to his every dare, including a trip to the altar in a twenty-four-hour break from reality.

But when Logan's father—and Willow's boss— discovers they are married, there is only one thing to do: pretend the marriage is real long enough to safeguard Willow's job and for Logan to prove he's up to managing the family business. But the more Willow gets to know Logan, the more she realizes that behind the adrenaline-addict facade there's a man she could fall for if she's not very careful indeed.

I loved getting to know Willow and Logan and spending time with them in Vegas, London and on the Massachusetts shore. I hope you do too!

Love,

Jessica

It Started with a Vegas Wedding

Jessica Gilmore

HARLEQUIN

Romance

(H) HARLEQUIN®

Romance™

Recycling programs
for this product may
not exist in your area.

ISBN-13: 978-1-335-73706-9

It Started with a Vegas Wedding

Harlequin Enterprises ULC
22 Adelaide St. West, 41st Floor
Toronto, Ontario M5H 4E3, Canada
www.Harlequin.com

Printed in U.S.A.

Incorrigible lover of a happy-ever-after, **Jessica Gilmore** is lucky enough to work for one of London's best-known theaters. Married with one daughter, one fluffy dog and two dog-loathing cats, she can usually be found with her nose in a book. Jessica writes emotional romance with a hint of humor, a splash of sunshine, delicious food—and equally delicious heroes!

Books by Jessica Gilmore

Harlequin Romance

The Princess Sister Swap

Cinderella and the Vicomte
The Princess and the Single Dad

Billion-Dollar Matches

Indonesian Date with the Single Dad

Fairytale Brides

Reawakened by His Christmas Kiss
Bound by the Prince's Baby

Mediterranean Fling to Wedding Ring
Winning Back His Runaway Bride
Christmas with His Cinderella
Christmas with His Ballerina

Visit the Author Profile page
at Harlequin.com for more titles.

For Sheila—the most insightful and patient
of editors

Praise for
Jessica Gilmore

"Totally loved every page. I was hooked right into
the story, reading every single word. This book has
to be my new favourite. Honestly this book is most
entertaining."

—*Goodreads* on *Honeymooning with
Her Brazilian Boss*

PROLOGUE

THE CROWD APPLAUDED as the groom swung the bride into his arms, the pair in complete tune with the music and with each other for one long, charged moment before they turned to beckon their friends and family to join them on the softly lit dance floor. Willow couldn't stop herself from looking up at Logan in entreaty—but whether it was an entreaty to join the dancing or to slip away before they were noticed she couldn't say. Probably both. She was divided, like every other moment of this long, strange day.

Long, strange and, she had to admit, exhilarating.

'Relax,' Logan said, the laughing note in his voice almost as hypnotic as the amused gleam in his dark blue eyes as he took her hand and led her onto the now crowded floor. 'What's the first rule of wedding crashing?'

'Pick a large, anonymous venue obviously

filled with work colleagues and second cousins?' Willow repeated his own words back to him, and Logan's smile widened.

'Clever girl. Now, rule number two, look like you belong.'

'I can't believe I am listening to you. I must have hit my head when I fell,' she said as much to herself as him.

His grip tightened around her waist, and Willow's stomach tumbled with the same terrifying mix of adrenaline and desire that had fuelled her all day. 'But you're having fun, admit it?'

'Yes.' The word was true, to her utter surprise. 'I am.'

'Then that's all that matters.'

For once Willow didn't point out that fun wasn't all that mattered at all. That responsibility and focus were the keys to stability and stability the key to happiness. Because today she wasn't sensible Willow Jones, dutiful and perennially worried daughter, sister and aunt, nor was she Willow Jones, high-flying Regional Finance Director, Europe. That Willow Jones was always professional, a woman who had spent the last four days getting up early to exercise before attending every session at the HartCo Directors' Conference, spending her evenings catching up on work alone in her room while her colleagues took every advantage of Las Vegas's tawdry charms. Not a woman playing hooky from the conference on a day when instead of instinctively saying no to anything outside her comfort zone, she forced herself to say yes.

Today, for one day only, she was allowing herself to explore the Willow she might have been if she hadn't been forced to grow up so soon, as carefree and impulsive as any of her family.

She closed her eyes and let Logan pull her close, swaying to the music, her body pressed enticingly close to his. She could feel the hardness of his thigh against hers, the muscles of his taut stomach and broad chest, the strength in his arms and she made herself relax, luxuriating in every millimetre of contact, her greedy body aching for more. In a day of wild adventures, his company was the wildest thing of all. She should have nothing in common with the playboy son of HartCo's CEO, a man better known for his adrenaline-filled lifestyle than his interest in the global company he would inherit one day, but the day had slipped by with laughter and easy conversation—and the occasional loaded silence.

Willow had thought she was immune to

Logan's kind of charm, had told herself that tousled dirty blond hair, amused blue eyes, easy smiles and a body toned to perfection by a life filled with surfing, sailing and other outdoor pursuits would leave her cold. She'd been wrong. The moment Logan had taken to the stage the first morning to officially open the conference in his father's stead, her body had sat up and taken notice. No, if she was honest, she'd developed a crush when she'd spied him in the London office the year before.

Still, she might have managed to continue ignoring the inconvenient attraction if Logan hadn't been the one to pull her back just as she was about to step out in front of a speeding car, the heat and noise of Vegas's centre confusing her into forgetting that here, cars drove on the right. The near miss had been far *too* near, the screech of brakes all she could hear, the smell of hot metal and oil encompassing her, the nose of the car filling her entire eyeline. For one terrifying moment, Willow had actually seen her life flash before her eyes. It had been uncomfortable viewing: a life filled with duty, a life devoid of adventure. A life she had chosen.

Her sister's words from the week before filled her brain: *You live life like it's a to-do list. Like ticking off things achieved will make you happy rather than ticking off things you do! Where's your sense of adventure, Willow? Your joy? I don't want you to one day realise you have all the security in the world but you have never lived.*

So here she was. Living. Saying yes to every wild scheme Logan could devise from that first lunchtime drink to help with the shock where, her guard ripped away by the cortisol and adrenaline still shooting round her body, she had accepted his challenge to experience Vegas through his eyes. Yes to the roulette wheel, to zip lines and helicopter rides, yes to crashing a wedding. Yes to a day of freedom from being Willow Jones. She had no idea why Logan had taken it upon himself to tutor her in risk-taking, but she wasn't going to look a gift horse in the mouth. Whatever that meant.

She raised her gaze to Logan's mouth and froze. It was framed by a strong jaw and neatly defined cheekbones, well-shaped, with an adorable indent above his top lip. She wanted to trace the lines of it, to press her finger into that indent, to taste it...

Time seemed to stop, the blood roaring in her ears, rushing around her body at warp speed. Her pulse was hammering, every nerve in her body at attention. She had never been so aware of her own physicality before, nor that of any other person. She could feel every single place where his body touched hers, heat blazing through her, need pooling hot and heavy and sweet in the pit of her stomach.

Somehow she forced her gaze upwards, to find it caught in his, the laughter fading from his eyes to be replaced by something darker, more primal. Nervous, she moistened her lips and felt his gaze dart to her own mouth.

This urgent need was more than she had ever handled before, and Willow didn't have the tools to manage it. This was nothing like the sensible and sedate dates she usually accepted, some of which lengthened into sensible and sedate relationships. This was raw and elemental and terrifying—and completely intoxicating. She wanted Logan to kiss her more than she had ever wanted anything before—and she was absolutely terrified of what would happen if he did. Somehow she managed to find some words, to rasp them out. 'I don't do one-night stands.'

His gaze grew even more hungry. 'Nor do I.'

She stared up at him, no longer moving, incapable of thought, and his smile grew, slow and sweet and very, very dangerous.

'So, Willow Jones,' he asked softly, 'what do you want to do next?'

CHAPTER ONE

LOGAN HARTWELL III shifted uncomfortably. Everything hurt from his little toenails to his pounding forehead. Something was beeping close by, the pitch the wrong side of comfortable as he prised open his eyes.

Where was he? There was something he had to do. Something important… He reached for it, but no. It slid away into the dull, grey haze that was his memory.

'Good. You're awake.'

If he had had the strength to sigh, Logan would have done so. The last thing he needed at any time, but especially when he had no idea where he was or why, was his father's disapproval. Although to be fair, that disapproval was a given no matter what his state.

Or his achievements.

The light hurt so much that when he finally managed to open his eyes enough to see, he immediately closed them again, before making the effort all over again. Shapes slowly firmed, and his chest tightened as Logan realised he wasn't in his apartment or a hotel room but a hospital. The beeping came from a monitor, and several wires connected him to various bits of medical paraphernalia.

What the hell?

Upright and uptight in the chair at the far side of the room sat Logan Hartwell II, mouth compressed, gaze unreadable.

Logan managed to resist the urge to ask where he was—or more importantly, why. There was no way he was giving his father any further advantage. 'Did you bring flowers?'

The only reaction was a thinning of already thinned lips. 'Do you know why you're here?'

Ah, he wasn't going to avoid the *why* question. Gingerly Logan tested his memory. Flashing lights, music, heat and laughter teased him, a sense of happiness, a hint of desire—more than a hint, but he couldn't hold on to any of it. 'Enlighten me.'

'You damn fool. When are you going to grow up? A man in your position can't afford to keep taking these risks. You could have killed yourself—you damn well nearly did— and your best friend is in an induced coma right now. I hope you're proud. Was the adrenaline high worth it, Junior?'

Logan didn't snap back 'Don't call me Junior' as he usually did. He couldn't say anything at all. Memories were coming back in dizzying waves. Paddling out, his mind distracted, not concentrating, not seeing Nate or hearing his shout of warning until it was too late. A collision, boards smashing together, Nate flying up into the air before crashing down on his board and sliding into the water, Logan submerged under the ocean, his mouth filling with salt and water as he yelled his cousin's name, trying to find him as the wave ruthlessly dragged him away.

A moment of distraction and he had nearly died. He had nearly killed his cousin and best friend. He couldn't even remember what had been so important it had taken his mind so dangerously off his game.

'How is he?' he croaked.

'They're waiting for the brain swelling to go down.' His father paused, and when he spoke again, his voice was gentler. 'But they're hopeful. They'll know more once they wake him up and can do a full neurological exam. The main worry is his spinal cord. If it's bruised then that may impact his mobility, possibly permanently. They don't think that's the case, but they can't rule it out. Either way, he'll probably need an operation, will have to stay in intensive care for some time and undergo a programme of rehabilitation when he gets home. I've told his parents not to worry, we'll take care of everything. But you are too old for me to have to clean up this kind of mess, Junior.'

Logan closed his eyes again, the guilt heavy and overwhelming. Ever since boyhood, Logan and Nate had been more like brothers than cousins. They looked out for one another, always. Logan knew better than to allow himself to be distracted when on a board, but he had broken that cardinal rule, and now Nate was paying the price. His throat closed. '*I'll* take care of it. It's my fault,' he managed. He was damned if he—or Nate—would be beholden to his dad in any way.

'I can believe that.' His father sighed, a familiar mix of exasperation and anger. 'Come on, Logan, what's it all for? When are you going to settle down? Take your responsibilities at Hartwell Corporation seriously? You're the heir to an empire. There are thousands of people all over the world whose livelihoods depend on a smooth succession one day. I never forget that running HartCo is both a great privilege and an even greater responsibility, but I've never seen that commitment in you. Instead you waste your time on your ridiculous project, on surfing and sailing and climbing and any other damn fool sport that endangers your life. It would break your grandfather's heart to see you squandering your life like this, to see you turning your back on his legacy.'

As Logan had been listening to a version of this speech for the last decade, he knew it wasn't worth retorting that his *ridiculous project* had a more than healthy turnover, that it employed dozens of people in Romney, their hometown on the north Massachusetts shore, that the boards and surf accessories, the sailing clothes and climbing gear his company produced were sold globally. His father didn't care. Compared to HartCo, even a healthy turnover was pocket money at best—and any commercial interest outside the family empire was heresy.

But the reference to his grandfather was new—and struck him hard. His grandfather had been supportive of Lona, the company Logan and Nate had set up after college, but Logan knew he had always assumed that it was a temporary distraction for Logan, an opportunity for him to stretch his wings and have some independence, to learn about business from the ground up before taking his rightful place at the head of the family empire. But for Logan, Lona was far more than an entrepreneurial apprenticeship for a man due to inherit a multimillion-dollar global company. It was the one place where Logan was himself, not the Hartwell heir or the disappointing son. It was a place that gave him the freedom to travel and pursue his passions, true, but just as importantly, it enabled him to be part of the town, the community. Part of the Byrne clan, not the Hartwell overlords.

And that his father would never understand. Logan tried to unset his jaw. 'I have never turned my back on HartCo or the family. Grandfather knew that. He was proud of Lona, proud of my sporting achievements.'

Unlike you.

'Achievements? You could have died, Logan.'

Was that *emotion* in his father's voice?

'I can't stand by and watch a careless accident happen again. This family has suffered enough unnecessary loss.'

'I know that, Dad.' His guilt intensified, a new and unwelcome empathy for his father joining it. It wasn't often that Logan Hartwell II mentioned Logan's mother. After her accident, almost every trace of her had been erased from the family house—and his father had done everything he could to erase any resemblance to his dead wife from his small son. It was a shame Logan's curling blond hair and blue eyes and his addiction to adrenaline-fuelled sports were a constant reminder of the woman his father couldn't tame.

Like mother, like son.

Logan had grown up knowing that nothing he did was good enough. If he got an A, his dad wanted to know why he wasn't top of the class, if he scored a basket why he hadn't been man of the match—and he had soon learnt not to discuss his surfing and sailing successes at home. The one thing he could do perfectly was disappoint his father, and it turned out that was a God-given talent he could manage without even trying. He was so used to it he had stopped caring about what his father thought a long time ago.

Or at least he tried to stop caring.

Over the next twenty-four hours, Logan's thoughts were as dark and tangled as his fitful drug-induced dreams as he waited to be discharged, desperate for news of Nate.

Please let him be all right, he prayed to a God he had long since stopped believing in. *I'll do whatever it takes to put this right.*

And in amongst the worry about his cousin, his father's words whirled round and round in his head. Much as it pained him to admit it, Logan could see that his father had a point.

He *could* have died out there in the ocean. After all, Nate was still in an induced coma. Logan had always enjoyed taking risks, but he had never come so close to his own mortality before. It was bound to make a man reassess.

And that reassessment was almost as painful as his bruises and scrapes, as his pounding head. He couldn't push the inconvenient truth aside any longer. It was time to face the fact that he had been treading water for the last couple of years. He was no longer the boy driven by anger and pride to start his own business whilst Lona was established enough for Logan to step away from the day-to-day management. But he couldn't evade his family obligations forever, nor deep down did he want to. After all, HartCo wasn't just his father's company, it was his grandfather's and great-grandfather's before that and so on, stretching back through a line of Hartwells heading back to the eighteenth century. Logan didn't want to be the Hartwell who broke that chain. That had never been his intention. He had just wanted to show the world—his father—who he was as a man before he settled down. To prove that he was more than just the heir, that he was a success in his own right.

Logan had long ago come to terms with

the knowledge that whatever he did, he would never see pride in his father's cold grey eyes, but despite himself, he had to admit part of him still harboured hope of forcing a grudging respect from the man. Maybe if they were working closer together, if he showed his father just what he was capable of, then one day it wouldn't be so grudging. The last decade had been a lot of fun. Often he managed his business remotely as he travelled from championship to championship, but those days were coming to an end. The accident proved that. He needed to settle down, swallow his pride and work closely with his father. Take on his legacy rather than create one.

But even as he drifted into an uneasy sleep, a niggling unease worried at his brain. There was something he was supposed to do, something important, but the more he grasped at it, the more it eluded him, and by the time the nurse came in to give him the welcome news that Nate was awake and asking for him, it had completely gone.

'Junior!'

Logan had barely had a chance to get out of his car when his father's summons rang down the drive. He tried and failed to suppress a sigh as the command was repeated.

It was barely a month since he'd been released from the Hawaiian hospital, and Logan was already wondering if he had set himself on an impossible quest. His father seemed harder to please than ever, if such a thing was possible. It didn't help that Logan was still feeling the mental and physical effects of the accident. He expected to be sore for some time after the battering his body had taken, but it was the short-term memory loss that most concerned his doctors. Still, as far as Logan was concerned, forgetting a couple of weeks of his life was a small price to pay. He would give an awful lot more than that to see Nate back to full health. The good news was that his cousin's spinal cord hadn't been injured, which meant a full recovery was expected. The bad news was that that full recovery was a long way away, and Nate would be undergoing a couple of operations followed by some serious rehabilitation work over the next few months.

Logan could make sure he paid for the best doctors and physios, but no amount of money could speed up the healing process or assuage his guilt. He just wished he could remember why he had been so distracted, explain what had happened. But he couldn't, try as he might, despite the insistent feeling there was something important he should be doing. Tantalising hints of memory danced just out of reach—laughter, touch, a feeling of coming home, but nothing solid, nothing concrete. He knew from piecing his diary together that he had spent a week small-boat racing in California, using the time there to meet with some stockists and some of the professional surfers and sailors Lona sponsored, before heading to Las Vegas for the annual HartCo Conference. He usually skipped the event, but it had been his idea to hold it away from Boston in Sin City, which meant he'd felt obliged to attend. He had gone straight to Hawaii after the conference.

But these were facts, not memories. The last day he had any concrete memory of was back here in Romney, arranging to meet Nate in Hawaii for a week of championship surfing and meetings. California, Vegas and Hawaii before the accident were a complete mystery, and of the accident itself, he only remembered the moment of collision. He winced. It wasn't a good look, the two founding directors of Lona, a premier surf brand, being involved in such a rookie accident. They had a lot of brand damage limitation to do on top of everything else. With Nate out of action and Logan starting to take his place in the global executive team at HartCo too, he could do with another ten hours in the day.

Or an ally.

'Good day?' he said as he walked into the library, refusing to let his frustration at being summoned like a child show in his face or his tone.

His father shuffled some papers, sitting back in the imposing chair behind the even more imposing desk, as if he had more important things to do than engage with his son. Once Logan would have been required to stand on the rug before him, waiting to take whatever criticism was about to be levelled his way. Today he dropped into an armchair and pulled out his phone, starting to scroll though his emails, to all appearances completely absorbed. Two could play games after all.

His father caved first. 'I was thinking...'

Uh-oh, he knew that deceptively silky tone of voice. 'Careful. I've heard that can be dangerous.'

'The accident. It was too close a call. I nearly lost you, Logan.'

Logan blinked in surprise. His father had shown concern at the hospital, true, but he had been an extreme version of his usual hard-to-please self ever since. This kind of emotive language was practically unheard of. Despite himself, warmth spread through him. 'I'll be more careful, Dad…' he began, but his father continued as if he hadn't spoken.

'You are the last Hartwell. If you died without a child, what would happen to the company? It's past time you settled down. A man your age needs a wife, kids. We need an heir.'

The warmth turned instantly to ice. It wasn't Logan his father had worried about losing, it was Logan's future sons—and he did mean sons—and the future of the company. Logan sat back, deceptively casual. 'We? Well, you're still under sixty. It's not too late for you to remarry and present me with a brother or sister, I guess.' He wasn't being completely facetious. Truth was, he'd never understood why his father had never remarried, especially with such an apparently unsatisfactory only child.

A flash of irritation was his father's only acknowledgement of Logan's words. 'I've started to look at some suitable candidates.'

It took Logan no little effort to refrain from rolling his eyes. *Suitable candidates?* He knew his father took his position seriously, but he sounded more like a medieval king than a CEO. 'And then we'll send an ambassador to swap portraits and negotiate a settlement?'

'Being married to someone in your position isn't easy, Logan. You need a woman who understands our world, is born to it. She needs to be intelligent, Ivy League of course, but also educated in our customs. A woman who can add value to our business, enhance our name.'

The subtext was clear. *Not a woman like your mother.* Not a wild surfer girl more at home behind her father's bar than a fundraising gala. No, Logan was expected to unite with an East Coast princess, descended from a long line of East Coast aristocrats, a woman with old money and an older name.

Was this the price of his father's respect? Was it worth it?

Logan searched for something to say, something to buy himself time, but for once he had nothing. Yes, he knew he was the last of the Hartwells, and yes, he knew that if the company was to stay in private hands then he needed children to inherit it, but the thought of a suitable marriage contracted only for name and background repelled him. At the same time, he couldn't help but remember that his father had done the opposite. He had married for love, and it had been a disaster.

And it wasn't as if Logan had ever met

any woman he had wanted to commit to. Far safer to keep things short and sweet, to stay on the move, not let anyone in. What if someone Logan truly cared about saw the same things in him his father did? What if he was only capable of provoking disappointment? Maybe it wouldn't hurt to look at his father's list. It wasn't as if he had to commit to marrying any of them, after all.

Marry?

The word echoed throughout his head, and he squeezed his eyes closed, pain crushing his skull. Why did that word evoke such strange emotions? That nagging sense that something was missing, that he had forgotten to do something vital, increased. What was it?

'The right kind of wedding to the right kind of woman is just the thing to relaunch you into society,' his father continued, and the pain intensified.

Marry. Weddings.

A sign, Walk-in Weddings Available, in bright neon lights. Where? When? He leaned forward, closing his eyes, trying to force the visions to solidify.

Vegas, of course! Memories returned in flashes: laughing hazel eyes, a light floral scent, a gentle touch. A chapel, a dare, a promise. He sat bolt upright, words spilling out with the speed of the days and weeks rapidly returning to his consciousness. 'There's a problem with your plan, Dad. I'm think I'm already married...'

And then he remembered—and as his father sat back in shock, Logan realised he should have kept his mouth shut. His Vegas wedding had been a momentary madness, something he should have undone weeks before. But as the colour returned to his father's cheeks and the first question—*who?*—was fired, Logan knew he—and his temporary bride—wouldn't be able to disentangle themselves from their marriage quite as easily as they had planned.

CHAPTER TWO

WILLOW JONES CHECKED her phone for the hundredth time that day, anticipation immediately plummeting to familiar disappointment. She didn't want to think about how many times she'd checked it over the last few weeks. How long did it take to get an annulment, for goodness' sake?

She'd done her research, and in Nevada, home of impulse weddings, a plea of not being in sound mind was an easy route to wiping out a regretted *I do*. And she *hadn't* been in sound mind. The very fact she had agreed to marry a virtual stranger attested to that. A virtual stranger who had promised that his expensive attorney would sort everything out, and all she would need to do was sign the papers. A virtual stranger she hadn't heard from since. Disquiet whispered through her. The silence and the delay didn't make any sense. Surely

Logan wanted the whole debacle put behind him as quickly as she did?

And that, she told herself firmly, was the only reason for her disappointment. No part of her was foolish enough to be hoping for a word from him, a sign that he was thinking of her. It had been a one-day-and-one-night only deal. They had both agreed on that. And if there was anything Willow was good at, it was following rules. It was bad enough she had allowed herself to deviate from the straight and narrow at all, even if it was for just twenty-four hours.

But what a twenty-four hours…

Maybe once she had signed the annulment, she would stop reliving it in her dreams. Stop seeing Logan's wicked smile and the devilish glint in his eyes as he dared her to give in to the impulsive side she had always denied even existed, to the instant attraction she should have known better than to trust. But then, she had never experienced anything like it before. No wonder her defences had been so quickly overcome. Not that she had put up much of a fight.

Somehow Willow managed a wry smile as she slipped her phone back into her pocket and continued walking along the familiar route that led from her flat to her sister's home; next time she married on impulse, she would at least make sure she had her groom's personal phone number first. But the smile quickly faded to be replaced by churning unease that had plagued her for the last few weeks. There was nothing Willow hated more than not being in control, not having an action plan. This patient waiting sat uneasily on her.

There was only one thing she could do. If Logan didn't contact her soon, she would have to use his work email to get in touch with him. But like all the executive team, he had an assistant guarding his inbox. Even a coded message would look odd—why would a UK-based regional director need to speak to a Hartwell? After all, there were several layers of senior management as well as an ocean between them. She hadn't met Logan in a meeting or an email chain before Vegas. The last thing Willow wanted was news of her mistake getting out at HartCo. Her reputation would be ruined, and she had worked so hard to get to where she was.

She turned onto her sister's street and pushed her own problems out of her mind as she saw Mia tear down the street to greet her.

'Aunty Willow, I'm so glad you're here!' As Mia neared, Willow could see how pale and pinched she looked. Willow held out her arms and embraced her small niece, holding her close. The worry in Mia's face tore at her. She knew that expression, what it was like to carry too much responsibility too young. But she'd never seen it mirrored in her seven-year-old niece before.

'Hello, sweetie, how was school?' She deliberately made light conversation as she followed Mia into the narrow hallway and up the stairs which led to her sister's flat.

Less than two years separated Willow and Skye, but their lives couldn't have been more different. Willow lived alone in a modern flat whereas Skye, at only twenty-eight, was already a mother of three. The family lived in an untidy but cheerful apartment above the vegan cafe Skye ran with her husband, Jack. Usually Willow could hear the children's chatter before she was halfway up the stairs, but today all was ominously quiet, the tension palpable. The unease that had gripped her the moment she had seen Mia's expression intensified, nudging her own stress about Logan's silence aside.

'Hi,' she said as brightly as she could as she pushed the apartment door open. 'It's me.'

'Aunty Willow!' Five-year-old Noah descended on her, followed by three-year-old Harper. She liked to think they were just glad to see her—but they knew she never arrived empty-handed.

'Let me see.' She pretended to rummage in her bag. 'What's this? I don't remember seeing these before.' She pulled out three books, a storybook for Mia, picture books for the other two. 'Who could have put these here?'

'The book fairy,' Harper breathed, wide-eyed, and Willow bent to kiss her small niece. 'It must have been. Why don't you look at the pictures, and I'll read them to you later? Hey,' she added to her sister, trying to hide her shock at the shadows under her sister's usually bright eyes, the lines in her normally smooth cheeks and forehead.

'You spoil them.' But the usual scold was mechanical.

'Technically the book fairy spoils them, but if it *was* me, isn't spoiling an aunt's job?' Willow loved being an aunt. She might have thought that twenty was far too young to get married and get pregnant, concerned that Skye was heading down the same irresponsible path their parents had blithely skipped down, but her sister was a great mother, the kids happy and well looked after. The cafe Skye and Jack ran had a good reputation and a respectable turnover. But that didn't mean Willow ever stopped worrying. She knew how precarious life could be with a young family and a small business. Which was why she had hurried to her sister's as soon as she possibly could. It was unlike Skye to ask for help—although that had never stopped Willow giving it.

'It's a job you do far too well. Tea—or wine?'

'Tea, please.' Willow followed Skye into the small galley kitchen. Barely big enough to hold two, it was, as usual, scrupulously clean, if haphazard. Willow liked everything neatly in its place. She could never fathom how her sister managed in such organised chaos. Skye put the kettle on and grabbed a mug for Willow, topping up her own still half-full glass of wine as she did so. Willow eyed her anxiously; her sister didn't usually drink in front of the children, a clear departure from their own upbringing.

'Everything okay?'

Skye set her glass down, chin wobbling, her mouth twisted in a clear attempt not to cry. 'No,' she managed at last.

'What is it? The kids? Jack? You're all well?'

'Yes, we're fine, health-wise at least.'

Willow's breathing eased, her chest loosening. 'Good, we can fix anything else.'

'It's this place. We've come to the end of the lease, and our landlord wants to put the rent up. He wants to double it, and we just can't afford it. Oh, Will. We're going to lose our home, our cafe, everything we have worked so hard for.'

Ten minutes later, Willow had installed the children in front of the TV while the adults sat around the small dining table at the other end of the sitting/dining room, keeping their voices low so as not to be overheard, although Willow noticed Mia sneaking anxious glances back at them.

'I guess you've checked the lease?' Willow asked, and Jack nodded.

'We're at a revise and renew phase. This area is a victim of its own success. When we opened up, it was still pretty gritty, but that made it affordable. Lots of local businesses opened, so more people wanted to move here, and so rents and house prices have risen astronomically.'

'People like you help make the area a place where people want to live, and then you get priced out as a thank-you.'

'I always meant to expand when the kids were older,' Jack said, his eyes as shadowed with exhaustion as his wife's. 'Start an evening bistro three nights a week, supply other cafes and shops with our bread and cakes. If I did that now, I think we could afford the increase, but it needs investment and time. New ovens, a redesign of the cafe, more staff...'

'And you working all hours,' Skye interrupted tearfully. 'We'd never see you.'

'Have you spoken to a bank?'

He nodded. 'But I have no collateral. We'd need to pay the increased rent straight off, then close for at least two weeks while we did the redesign, hired more people and get the equipment. We'd need a buffer for the first three months while we established the new business.'

'So you need, what?' She did a rapid mental calculation. 'Twenty-five...thirty thousand?'

'At least. I'll never lay my hands on that amount. But I know I could make a go of it. That's what's so frustrating.'

As Willow walked the short distance back to her flat, her head whirled with a dizzying mix of emotions. Sadness that her sister and family faced this impossible situation, anger at the landlord for putting them there, and a bitter streak of memory. She'd seen her own childhood reflected in Mia's expression—although at least Skye and Jack were facing up to the problem and not running away from it as her parents had always done. She was also conscious of a Cassandra-like guilt, that her exhortations to be careful, warnings that small businesses were a notoriously risky venture, had been proved right.

And guilt that she hadn't immediately offered to help.

Willow slowed as she reached the canal path and turned onto it. Pretty Victorian cottages lined the path, doors in myriad shades of bright and pastel colours, shutters at the windows, tiny front gardens blooming with flowers. Estate agents' signs stood in two front gardens.

The cottages were, like all London property, ludicrously priced, especially as the front door opened straight into the small sitting room, with a kitchen diner at the back and one good-sized bedroom upstairs, the second fit only for a study, and neither of the houses for sale had converted their attic. But ever since she had been small, Willow had dreamed of living in one of these houses. They had represented a fairy-tale-type security in a childhood filled with insecurity. And she was so close to achieving that dream…

Her flat had doubled in value, ironically because of the same gentrification that was impacting Skye. She was expecting a huge bonus again, and her savings were healthy thanks to her habit of tucking away all her bonuses and at least ten per cent of her salary plus whatever was left at the end of the month. The mortgage advisor had seemed confident she could borrow what she needed on top, and so she had booked an appointment to look around both cottages this very weekend.

Her savings were healthy enough to advance Jack and Skye all the money they needed.

She knew she would, and willingly too. *Of course* she would. It was just she wasn't ready to say goodbye to her dream quite yet. Let her have the night to be selfish and mourn the loss of her fantasy house. Then tomorrow she would give Skye the good news that the family were safe. And then she needed to sort out her own mistakes. Embarrassment or not, she was tracking Logan Hartwell down and putting the whole twenty-four hours they had spent together firmly in the past. Skye's situation was a stark reminder that fantasy and dreams weren't for her. They never had been. Too much depended on Willow being the sensible one. That was what was important, not impulsive adventures or being swept off her feet. No, from now on, Willow's feet were staying firmly on the ground, no matter how irresistible the temptation.

Logan halted at the entranceway to the apartment block, doubt replacing the clarity of purpose that had propelled him through the last twenty-four hours. He inhaled, rapidly calculating as he realised there were still far too many unknowns to ensure a successful outcome to the scheme he had rapidly come up with, Willow's reaction most of all. After all, he had promised her a speedy annulment. Now here he was, on her doorstep, to ask her to change the terms of their temporary agreement.

But thanks to Logan blurting out their secret in front of his father, he wasn't sure what choice either of them had. Logan Hartwell II wasn't a man who suffered fools gladly, and spin it as he might, there was no doubt an impulse wedding entered into for one night only was foolish. Unforgivable behaviour in a son already marked as unreliable, it would guarantee there would never be any chance of fixing their relationship, even if Logan worked twenty-four hours a day whilst fathering ten suitable heirs. But as his father still needed Logan, it was all too likely he would take out the bulk of his anger on Willow. This incident could tarnish Willow's career, maybe irreparably. Logan had got her into this mess. Now he had to get her out of it, whether she liked it or not.

Willow Jones lived in a modern block of flats, all gleaming glass and chrome, a little out of place in what was clearly a gentrifying part of London where bookies and pound shops rubbed shoulders with delis and interior design shops. The double doors at the entrance had been left ajar, and so Logan walked straight into the soulless lobby and headed to the lift, selecting the top floor. His mouth curved as he pressed the button. The penthouse? Willow might just fit in with the Hartwells after all.

The lift opened onto a corridor as soulless as the lobby with its generic faux marble tiles, white-and-grey walls, and some kind of chrome art motif repeated at regular intervals. There were eight apartments on the corridor, Willow's at one end. Logan didn't allow himself any more thinking time. Instead he strode purposefully to the pale wood door and knocked. There was no answer.

Now what? He deliberately hadn't called in advance or used the intercom downstairs to announce his arrival, not wanting to concede the advantage of surprise, but in his haste he hadn't allowed for the fact she might not be in. The last thing he wanted was to have this conversation in the office. Logan knocked again. No answer.

He blew out a breath. Purpose and focus had driven him here. He didn't want or need thinking time to derail him. He especially didn't want time to re-examine his newly regained memories of Vegas, those visceral recollections of heady attraction and mind-blowing instant connection. Those memories could only distract from what had to be a sensible, mutually agreed business proposition for both their sakes. Things were complicated enough without adding extra benefits in, no matter how tempting those benefits might be.

At that moment, a beep announced the arrival of the lift. Logan turned as the doors slid open and a young woman stepped out. Remembered desire shivered through him as she came into view. Tall, as slim as her name implied, brown hair pulled back in a knot, with clear hazel eyes, Willow halted several metres away, eyes wide with shock.

She folded her arms, eyes narrowed. 'Could this day get any worse?'

Logan blinked. He hadn't expected a rapturous reception, but this seemed a little extreme. 'Hello, Willow. You didn't write, you didn't call...'

Contrary to what anyone might expect, Logan hadn't been drunk the day he met—and married—Willow Jones. Tipsy by the end, sure. Champagne would do that to a man, but not drunk. In fact, contrary to what most people thought, Logan didn't drink much at all. Adrenaline was his drug of choice. Now his memory had returned, he had a full recollection of the less than twenty-four hours he'd spent with the woman standing in the corridor, arms crossed defensively, worry and suspicion lurking in long-lashed eyes. She'd been acerbic, yes, witty and clever, but full of a devil-may-care fire. A fire he had seen smouldering and deliberately stoked with explosive consequences.

There was no hint of that fire now, no humour in her direct gaze. 'Why are you here, Logan? You better have those annulment papers with you. Unless...' Her mouth twisted, allowing the vulnerability he had sensed in Vegas to peep through her stern facade. 'Has anyone found out about us? About what we did?'

Logan was suddenly weary, the jet lag—or the last month—finally catching up with him. 'Maybe we should discuss this inside?'

Willow didn't answer, but she walked past him and opened the door. When she didn't close it in his face, Logan took that as an invitation.

'Nice place,' he said as he stepped into the open-plan living area. Willow's flat was a corner apartment with a wraparound terrace. One side looked down on some cottages and a pretty enough canal, the other on the landscaped apartment gardens, sterile and devoid of anything resembling wildlife but better than the car park and road views her neighbours would enjoy. He quickly scanned the room. An L-shaped sofa and chair in a neutral grey linen, filled bookcases along one wall, tall stools at the kitchen island which partitioned the room. There were a few paintings on the wall—originals, not prints—and some framed photos of a woman who looked a little like Willow and what must be her family. None of Willow herself.

'Tea?'

'Good to see the national stereotypes are alive and well. No, thanks.' She still hadn't unbent to offer him as much as half a smile. 'Water though, if you can manage that.'

She raised an eyebrow, but when the water came, it did so with ice and lemon, and she had emptied some tortilla chips into a bowl, along with a plate of olives and a couple of dips.

Logan dropped onto the sofa and helped himself to an olive. 'Been here long?'

'About four years.' She stood straight-backed and unsmiling behind a chair, seemingly in control, but her hands as they gripped the seat back were white-knuckled, a sign of repressed inner emotion. 'Cut the small talk, Logan. Where are the papers? I've been out of my mind with worry. You promised that they would be with me straight away. I never would...' She faltered and looked at her hands.

It didn't take much to finish the sentence. 'Never would have married me without a get-out.' It was completely reasonable. After all, they didn't actually know each other, so Logan wasn't sure why her hurry to be rid of him cut quite so deep. It would just be nice for someone to want him, not want to change him or get something from him. And that night had been special, different to any relationship he had enjoyed before. Had the synchronicity between them been one-sided, Logan seeing what he wanted to see, not what was there? 'I know what we agreed, but before I got a chance to put things in motion, I was in an accident. There was some short-term memory loss, and I only remembered that we even *were* married yesterday. I hope you've not been too worried.'

She flushed with evident relief. 'That's good, not that you were in an accident obviously, I hope you are okay now, but good that you're able to fix things. I didn't expect you to come in person, though. An email would have been fine to put my mind at rest.'

'The thing is,' he said slowly, trying to find the right words, 'there's been a complication.'

She froze. 'A complication?'

'Maybe you should sit down.'

She stared at him for a long second before taking a chair facing the sofa, picking up her cup of tea, hands cradling it as if for comfort. 'Explain the complication. Won't they grant the annulment? What can we do about it?'

'Willow, I haven't actually put in for the annulment yet.'

'Then what…' She set her cup down. 'I was right. Someone knows.' It was a statement, not a question, and he nodded. She closed her eyes and sat back, pale now. When she opened them, her expression was bleak. 'How? I haven't said a word to anyone.'

'It was my fault,' he said grimly. 'I was with my father when my memory partially came back, and I blurted it out. I am so sorry.'

'Your father? Oh, my God.' She pressed her hand to her mouth, visibly fighting for control before pulling herself together, her expression unreadable. 'Am I sacked?'

'No.' Logan drew in a deep breath. 'At least, not yet. Willow, I am going to fix this, but I had to buy us time. You understand that, don't you? We can salvage this, but we have to work together.'

'How? How is this salvageable? I should never...' Again she bit the words back, and again he filled in the blanks, silently this time, but they echoed around the room anyway. *I should never have married you.* Not for the first time, Logan cursed the accident that had brought them here. If only they could have left their whirlwind romance as a special memory, rather than dealing with the fallout. But there was no point in recriminations. He had to concentrate on persuading her to agree to his proposition.

Just as she had agreed to every proposition back then. With an effort, he pushed the thought away. Things had changed too much. He didn't have the luxury of being the devil-may-care tempter any more, and this Willow was different too. She had retreated back into her shell, her pulled-back hair, severe trouser suit and remote expression a reminder that

Vegas was a different world. It was better this way, even as his memory ruthlessly reminded him of how silky her hair felt under his fingertips, bunched in his fists, of exactly what was under that buttoned-up suit. If this was to work, they had to stay focused. This time any dealings together had to be business, nothing else.

'Look, Willow.' Logan had spent the last twenty-four hours wondering how to handle this conversation, realising in the end that the only way was to be honest with her. After all, the day they had spent together had been grounded in honesty as well as adrenaline. 'My father and I have a difficult relationship.' He smiled wryly. 'And that's the understatement of the century. As far as he's concerned, I'm an impulsive fool not fit to bear the Hartwell name, let alone run the company.'

She frowned. 'But you have a great track record. I thought your own company was successful...'

'To him it's chicken feed and a distraction. The accident I was just in just confirmed his view. There are times when I want to walk away from him, his unrealistic expectations, his criticisms, but regardless of what he thinks and says, I am a Hartwell.' He stopped. The last thing he wanted to admit was how much he longed to see pride and respect in his father's eyes. 'The accident brought things to a head. My cousin, Nate, was badly injured, but it could have been a lot worse for both of us. Things are at a delicate point between me and my father right now. If he knew the truth about you and me, then it would destroy what little relationship we do have—forever.' Said out loud it sounded so melodramatic, but Logan knew it was nothing but the truth.

'The accident also made me realise it's time I faced up to my future responsibilities seriously, so I've taken up a role in the executive team at HartCo. The time is right. I'm not going anywhere, which means my father and I have to work together for the good of the company and everyone in it. I can't spend the next ten years at war with him. It's not good for HartCo.'

'I see that. But…'

'And then there's you,' he cut her off, needing to finish saying what he had come here to say. 'He can't disinherit me, much as he might want to, but he would definitely take his anger out on you. He could make your life very difficult, Willow, and I wouldn't put it past him. I won't let that happen. I won't let you pay for my family dramas.'

'I see.' Her mouth trembled. 'So how on earth can we fix this?'

Logan held her gaze as firmly as he could. 'We change the narrative. We own the wedding…we own the marriage.' He took a deep breath before saying for the second time, 'Willow Jones, would you do me the honour of being my wife?'

CHAPTER THREE

LOGAN'S WORDS HUNG in the air, an echo of the words he had used just over five weeks before. Willow could do nothing but stare at him, her mind whirling in panic.

What have I done?

If only she hadn't argued with Skye, if only she hadn't stepped out in front of that speeding car, if only it hadn't been Logan who pulled her back, if only she hadn't told him what Skye had said, if only she hadn't agreed to his proposition to cram a lifetime of experiences into one day.

If only he hadn't whisked her away on the most adrenaline-filled, unexpected day of her life.

If only she hadn't wanted him so very much.

If only she hadn't told him that she didn't do one-night stands. Because whom was she kidding? She had been so keyed up with frustrated desire, she would have agreed to an hour with him, let alone a night. Instead, the moment they passed a traditional Vegas chapel, one with pictures of an Elvis impersonator outside and a Walk-in Weddings Available sign, it had felt as if that was where they had been heading since the first contact. Logan had obviously felt the same way, because, eyes gleaming with desire, with challenge, he had actually gone down on one knee.

And there had been no other answer but yes. For that night alone.

At least, it was supposed to be.

She looked at Logan, outwardly calm and relaxed, sprawled on her sofa as if he belonged here with her, just as she had imagined too many times over the last month, much as she had tried not to. Did he regret it as much as she did? Stupid question. He had just spent eight hours on a flight to try and salvage both her career and his relationship with his father. Of course he did.

It isn't fair, she wanted to rage. She was usually so good, she followed the rules, she *set* the rules—that day in Vegas was the one time she had allowed herself to be impulsive in a lifetime of being the sensible one. Karma really didn't pull its punches.

Willow swallowed, gathering her emotions and squashing them down tightly, the way she always did, starting to formulate a plan instead. There was no point indulging in if-onlys and complaining to the fates. What mattered was what happened next.

'It wasn't supposed to be real,' she said almost to herself at last.

'No, but the wedding had real, legal consequences. We knew that at the time.'

And she had. She had just not allowed herself to consider what would happen if the annulment hadn't gone as smoothly as they had planned. Willow forced herself to focus, pushing the last of the panic down with her regrets as she tried to get some control back from the situation. 'What do you mean by changing the narrative?'

Logan leaned forward and picked up his water, and she got the sense he was choosing his words carefully. If she wasn't the carpe diem Willow of that day in Vegas, then neither was he the devil-may-care companion who had whisked her from adventure to adventure. How bad had the accident been? He was paler despite the year-round tan, new lines around his eyes, his cheeks a little hollower than five weeks before. Last time she had been with him, she had explored his face with her fingertips, with her mouth, run her hand down those cheeks, nibbled her way along his jawline, kissed him and been kissed until she didn't know where she began and he ended. She curled her fingers into fists, even as her body pulsed with the memory. How had she thought such unbridled passion could be consequence-free?

'Hear me out before you say anything, okay?'

Warily she nodded. She'd learned her lesson where letting Logan Hartwell sweet-talk her was concerned.

'I told my father that the wedding was planned. That we have been secretly dating for the last year and decided to get married in Las Vegas. But that we were trying to figure out what came next, as your job and family are based here and are so important to you. I also told him that because you work for HartCo, you were very keen to keep the marriage a secret until we'd decided where we were based and what came next.'

Willow made herself stay calm, not react in any way as she tested every one of his words, looking for loopholes and weak spots, despite an instinctive anxiety combined with a shameful and quickly smothered joy that their story wasn't yet done. 'But what about the last few weeks? Secret marriage or not, wouldn't I have tried to get in touch with you? Come over once I heard about the accident?'

'We kept the news of the accident quiet— no one mentioned it at work, did they? So there was no reason for you to hear about what happened.'

'But surely I would have messaged you, called you at some point? And…' Her brain continued to analyse the situation as if it were a spreadsheet. 'You might have forgotten we were married, but you didn't lose all your memory, did you? Wouldn't you have remembered we were dating and got in touch?' It wasn't that she didn't appreciate his attempt to help her—and himself—out of a sticky situation, but his cover story was full of as many plot holes as one of Mia's long stories.

'I've done a lot of reading about amnesia since the accident, and it's quite possible I could have forgotten about the whole relationship not just the marriage. But to make sure we were completely covered, I told my father that I had agreed to give you some space. I wanted to tell everybody about the wedding the next day. You had some regrets about eloping and what our future looked like and asked for time to think it through. We quarrelled and I stormed off to Hawaii, telling you that you had all the time you needed. But I realised yesterday that life was too short for us not to be together, and I came here to convince you to come back to Boston with me and to give our marriage a real go.' He looked ridiculously pleased with himself. Willow had to admit that he had thought quickly, but his solution created as many, if not more, problems than it solved.

'But I was promoted within the last year!' she said at last. 'It was quick, and I am young for the role. People will think that it was because I was dating you, that I didn't earn it on my own merits.' How could he, heir to a global family business, know how much self-sufficiency meant to her? How proud she was of her achievements?

And she didn't want to go back to Boston and live with him! She had a job and a life she was happy with. It was small and contained, but that was her choice. If she agreed, she wouldn't just have to share a home with him, but she would be scrutinised as the wife to the Hartwell heir. Everyone would be talking about them—especially her colleagues. Logan didn't know how much she liked her privacy and solitude, that a childhood moving from place to place, always different in clothes and name and lifestyle, meant that all she wanted was to slip under the radar. 'And

it's all lies,' she half whispered. 'We're not...
you don't want...how could we pull this off
even if I wanted to?' Madcap schemes, wild
plans, lies. They were her parents' stock in
trade, not hers.

Besides, if one night with him could turn
her life upside down, what would happen
if they were in close proximity for weeks,
months even? She had barely been able to
function just standing next to him. How
would she manage living with him? Sharing
a room with him?

'I'm sorry, Willow. If I could turn back
time...' Some of the arrogant confidence left
him, and he seemed to look straight past her.
'Well, there are lots of things I'd change. But
we are where we are, and the truth could end
your career. A few white lies seem allowable
under the circumstances.'

Willow shook her head. The whole conversation was absurd. 'Surely your father doesn't
believe any of it?'

'He couldn't believe that someone as intelligent as you would marry someone like
me.' For a moment she saw a flash of hurt,
and then it was gone as if it had never been.
'You're not who he had in mind as a Hartwell bride, but he's not as displeased as he
could be, considering this landed on him with

no warning. Apparently your reputation precedes you.'

'So, what does this mean? We delay the annulment?' Her stomach tightened. More uncertainty.

'We scrap the annulment idea. Then in a year or so, we agree that we made a mistake after all and get a nice tidy divorce. After all…' He smiled at her then, sweet and intimate. 'We *are* still married. I'm just asking you if we can stay that way for a bit longer, only together, not apart. I'll make it more than worth your while.'

Willow gulped her now lukewarm tea, wishing she'd opened a bottle of wine, her mind working rapidly. The last thing she wanted was to become embroiled in some elaborate pretence. But she could see that there was no way she would walk away from this scandal unscathed, that it was all too likely she would find herself without a job, her reputation tarnished. She'd pull herself up eventually, start again if she had to, but then what would become of her sister? She needed to be solvent to help Skye and her family, not out of work and unemployable.

'I'm talking about a year, Willow. It's not long, not in the grand scheme of things.'

She bit her lip. 'I don't know…it all seems

so unnecessarily complicated. Can't you tell him we decided we're better off as friends now and get the annulment as planned?'

'If that's what you really want, then of course. But…' He broke off.

'But?' she prompted.

'But if we did that, then we're still tarnished by the wedding in my father's eyes. He'll think us both flighty and indecisive. I'm used to that. I want to prove him wrong, but if you really don't want to do this, I'll take my medicine. I just don't want him to take it out on you. This way my father gets a chance to get to know you, so when we split up, your career and reputation aren't impacted.'

They'd come full circle, and much as she assessed, reassessed and moved things around, she couldn't see another way forward that left her gainfully employed with her reputation intact.

'One thing we didn't discuss is a prenup,' Logan added. 'We didn't need one because we planned an annulment, but if we are going to stay married, then it's something to consider. If you agree to this, Willow, I will make it worth your while.'

'I don't need your money.'

'Think of it as a bonus for a job well done.

A million on completion of a year of marriage.'

'Pounds or dollars?' she threw back at him, but he only smiled.

'Whichever you prefer.'

Willow got slowly to her feet and wandered over to the window, looking down at the canal and the pretty houses that overlooked it. A million pounds? That was a lot of money. The kind of money that would enable her to buy her dream home mortgage-free. Security in return for a year of her life? That was a price worth paying surely.

Especially as it wasn't her own security that was preying on her mind. She could wipe the worry off Mia's forehead with the word *yes*. Give her family a home and business no one could take away.

How could she not?

She turned to look at him directly, resolutely ignoring the way his hair flopped over his forehead, the tiredness in his eyes she wanted to kiss away, the arm flung across the back of the sofa as if waiting for her to curl up into it. She couldn't allow emotion anywhere near this decision, not this time. 'How about instead of the million, you buy a building— a specific building—including the lease. You let the current tenants live there rent-free all year, and then at the end of the year, you sign the building over to them.'

She held her head high. With no rent to pay Jack could start to make all the improvements he wanted. Her sister and her nieces and nephew would be safe.

Logan's smile was sweet and sure. He knew he had her, and her pulse thudded at the thought. She made herself breathe deep and slow, steadying herself, focusing on the negotiation, not the insistent urge of her body. 'Is this building a billion-dollar office block? I need more info than that, Willow.'

'It's a three-storey building around the corner, a cafe with a maisonette upstairs. Property prices are going up fast round here, and I don't know how much the building plus freehold will be. It might be more than a million, it might be less. But that's my price.'

'I see.' He smiled then, and despite all her best endeavours, Willow lost her ironclad grip on her emotions just for a moment, her body reminding her with a jolt just how lost she'd been in those navy-blue eyes, how she'd wanted him to smile at her with approval. With an effort, she forced herself to recall the flip side, how reckless and impulsive she had been. How dangerously addictive the fun had been. Did she really want to spend a year married to this man? Did she dare?

Logan got to his feet, the languid grace disguising his strength. He held out a hand. 'Deal.'

Willow stared at his hand, unsure whether it was offering her salvation or damnation. 'I won't say deal until I see the postnuptial agreement and the deeds to the building,' she said at last. 'But if they look satisfactory, then I am looking forward to working with you.'

'Likewise. We make a good team, Willow Jones.' He took her hand in his, and the sensation and memory of his touch engulfed her.

She dropped his hand and backed away hurriedly. Her body still hummed with need, hot and sweet and dangerous. She had to put a stop to it. She couldn't lose herself again.

'One more condition,' she said hurriedly. 'We may be married legally, but that doesn't mean we are married in any way that matters. Let's keep things uncomplicated.'

'Uncomplicated?'

'Separate beds. This is a business arrangement, after all.'

'Of course.' His expression was completely inscrutable.

'Good, glad we're on the same page.'

'Me too. I'll be in touch, but start getting

your things in order. I'd like us to leave within the week.'

And with a nod he was gone, leaving Willow standing staring after him, unsure what she had just agreed to, unsure as to why. But one thing she did know. Logan Hartwell was trouble, and she was in way over her head.

'A private jet?' Logan couldn't tell whether Willow was overwhelmed or disapproving as the security guard conveyed her into the comfortable seating area of the plane he had chartered to take them home.

He stood up, leaving his laptop on the sofa, where he'd been reading through his emails as he waited for Willow to board. 'It's more convenient than a commercial airline. Besides, we need to talk freely, and I would rather we weren't overheard.' A talk that was long overdue, but his wife had been elusive over the last week.

His wife. Logan wasn't sure he would ever get used to the word.

Willow nodded slightly but didn't move any further into the cabin, standing with one hand on the door, as if she were poised to run away from him and this suddenly all-too-real marriage.

Maybe he'd join her. This was it. There was no turning back.

'How was your family?'

'Jack and Skye still can't believe their reprieve. It's all they can talk about.' All her sister knew was that Willow had offered to take over the rent, and happy-go-lucky Skye had accepted the news unquestioningly.

'You haven't mentioned the rest?'

She flushed slightly. 'No. I wasn't sure what to do. Skye and I, we don't lie to each other. But I don't want her to feel under an obligation to me, so I told her the same thing I told my colleagues, just that I've been offered a year's secondment to Boston with a large enough payrise to enable me to take over the rent. It wasn't easy saying goodbye to the children, though.' She swallowed and looked down, and Logan did his best to ignore the sliver of hurt caused by her words. It wasn't personal that she hadn't mentioned him to her family. She was just keeping things simple. It was the right decision, as was her request they occupy separate beds, stay married in name only. Sharing even some of his life with another person would be exposing enough. It was good to know there were limits.

And hopefully in time he would stop noticing how attractive she was, stop remembering the way she felt, the sounds she made, the way she tasted. And those thoughts weren't helping at all.

'Come on,' he said. 'Let me show you around.'

'This plane is bigger than where I grew up,' she said at last as she left one of the two en suite double bedrooms. With a jolt, Logan realised the reality of the situation, that he didn't know this woman at all. He'd been so caught up in the practicalities of first persuading Willow to agree and then getting her to the States that he hadn't had time to consider the reality of spending a year with someone who was actually a near stranger.

But that year was about to begin, and ready or not, they were bound together.

He studied her discreetly as she buckled herself in for take-off. She had good manners, thanking the stewardess as she checked in on them, seemed calm as she took everything in, not over-impressed or overawed by the luxury even though it was clearly new to her.

What else did he know about her? Willow was obviously very good at her job, a regional director whilst still in her twenties. Family-oriented—it hadn't taken him long to discover that her sister rented the building he had bought, nor that the rent had been due to be drastically increased. In the end it hadn't been money or the potential loss of reputation that had pushed Willow into agreeing to this year. It was the opportunity to help her sister. He understood that. After all, he would do anything to help Nate.

She was beautiful, although more severe than in Vegas. Then her hair had fallen around her face in soft waves, and she'd worn a long yellow sundress that had clung to every curve. This Willow, like the one in her apartment, was contained. Her make-up was minimal, her hair tied back. She exuded an air of formality in tailored jeans and a cashmere cardigan and top, discreet studs in her ears and a locket around her neck her only adornment. There was very much a hands-off vibe to her, a reminder of the business relationship she had determined their marriage should be.

She was right, it was certainly safer. They may have had undeniable chemistry in Vegas. But look at the trouble that had got them into.

Neither spoke during the safety briefing, nor during take-off, Willow reading as Logan watched London disappear beneath them.

Logan waited until the pilot announced they were cruising and could move around the cabin before turning to Willow, who, although she appeared absorbed in her book, had turned very few pages. 'I've organised for some drinks and food to be served now,' he said. 'I think this would be a good time for us to talk, don't you?'

Willow slowly closed the book, her gaze faraway and distracted, before clearing as she nodded decisively. 'Of course,' she said as agreeably as if he'd asked her for some figures.

A few moments later, they were ensconced in the seating area, Willow selecting the armchair opposite the sofa. Logan dropped onto the sofa, thanking the stewardess as she brought a tray laden with small sandwiches, fruit, scones and small cakes. 'I thought you might appreciate an afternoon tea,' he said. Willow just stared at him for a second. Then a vivid smile transformed her face. Logan's breath caught. There it was: the fire that turned a rather austere prettiness into real beauty.

'My last taste of England?'

'Something like that.'

They ordered their drinks, and once everything was served, Logan dismissed the stewardess waiting until she exited the seating area before sitting back and regarding his wife. 'We have a history to establish. Where do you want to start?'

'At the beginning, I guess. How did we meet?'

'I was in London for a week or so, last year. We must have been in the office at the same time then.'

'We were,' she said quietly.

How had he not noticed her? But then, Logan was aware that Willow was very good at blending into the background when she wanted to. After all, he hadn't noticed her at the conference either, with her sensible suits and pulled-back hair, not until he had pulled her out of the way of a too-fast car, and in the shock she'd dropped her facade.

'Perfect. We met in London. I took you out to dinner a few times…'

'And I took you out. To an art exhibition, the opera.'

'This is meant to be believable, remember?'

'Cultural enrichment is a two-way process.' Her smile was full of mischief, and Logan's blood began to heat. Damn, but he liked it when she provoked him.

'You better send me details of the exhibition. I can claim to have slept through the opera. Then we had weekend breaks together whenever I was in Europe. I'll send you the dates, but mostly we video-called, late into the night.'

'Not too late. I'm a responsible employee, remember?'

'Of course. And so we continued until a few weeks ago when reunited in Vegas we realised we wanted to be together properly, no more snatched moments.'

'You're good. You should do this for a living.'

'I talked you into marriage, but then the next day you realised it had all been a bit too sudden and that you needed some time.'

She nodded, her forehead furrowed in concentration. 'That works. Okay, what did we talk about during those late-night conversations? Give me a quick rundown of the life and times of Logan Hartwell.'

'Logan Prestwood Hartwell III, actually. Okay. I'm thirty. My birthday is in August. My mother died when I was five in a riding accident.'

'I am so sorry.' Her hazel eyes were dark with sympathy. 'You're an only child, aren't you? That must have been lonely.'

'It could have been,' he admitted gruffly. 'Luckily, we lived with my paternal grandparents, and I was very close to my grandmother in particular. And my mother was a local girl. Her parents owned the local Inn in Romney, the town I grew up in and still live in, and her brother, Nate's dad, took it over, so I had her family close at hand. Nate and I are more like brothers than cousins.'

'And your dad didn't remarry?'

'No. He didn't even really date afterwards, let alone get near to marriage.'

'He must have loved your mother very much.'

'You'd think so, but all I remember is arguments between them. Growing up, every criticism seemed to be how like her I was.' Logan didn't really want to dwell on any of that ancient history. 'Okay, that's pretty much it. I went to the local school until middle school and then to a prep school a few towns over and was shipped off to boarding school my freshman year of high school, the same one my father and paternal grandfather attended. You work for HartCo, so you probably don't need a recap on the history of it.'

'I've read the corporate literature,' she agreed. 'HartCo, officially Hartwell Corporation, is one of the oldest privately owned businesses in the States with roots going back pre-Independence. Over the centuries it's expanded into a huge media conglomerate with offices around the globe, including London, Sydney, and several non-English-speaking territories as well. Your father is the current owner, proprietor and CEO.'

'That's an A for you. One thing you really need to understand is that we are an old New England family, and that is something my father takes very seriously. To many of my ancestors' annoyance, there were no Hartwells on the Mayflower, although we married into plenty of families who were, but we were still early settlers in Boston. Over the years the company has grown, run into trouble, grown again depending on which particular Hartwell was in charge. But somehow over the years the family has shrunk, my father the only Hartwell of his generation and me of mine.'

'It must be a huge responsibility,' Willow said softly. 'All that history.'

'Don't be fooled by the company propaganda. It's a varied history—for every upstanding, hard-working patriarch, there have been plenty of profligates and scandals, seduction, fraud, affairs and even murder. A family as old and rich as ours has more than its fair share of skeletons.'

'That would liven up the corporate literature. Okay, tell me about your own company. Lona, isn't it?'

'Not the most original of names...'

'Better than Nagon. I assume that was the other option?'

Logan laughed. 'Luckily we didn't get that far. Nate found out that Lona as a Hungarian girl's name means *light*, and the decision was made.'

'Pretty.'

'It also means *canvas* in Spanish, but we didn't realise that at the time. Lona is about nine years old as an incorporated business, but it has its roots back to when we were fifteen, when Nate and I started up a summer beach supply business, selling wetsuits, floats, things like that. We learned to make our own surfboards around the same time and got some requests to make some for other people. Word of mouth spread, and soon we had a waiting list. There was no grand plan or anything, but by the time we graduated college, we were making decent money each summer, and so we decided to see what would happen if we ran with it. Now we employ around eighty people at the headquarters in Romney, some in manufacturing, some in distribution or marketing. It's the biggest town employer outside tourism.'

'Impressive,' she said, but her forehead was crinkled. 'Is Romney in Boston? I thought that's where you lived?'

'About thirty miles north. Just before the turn of the last century, my great-great-grand-father moved out of the city to what was then a small oceanside settlement. We've lived there ever since. Several generations of Hartwells under one roof, working, living and feuding together.' He watched realisation dawn on her face.

'Under one roof? Still? You live in the same house as your father? *We* will be living with him?'

He nodded. 'I've spent most of the past decade travelling around to get away from my father, but yes, when in Romney, I live at Lookout House.' It wasn't that he hadn't thought of getting his own place, but Lookout House was his home, and he loved every inch of it. Moving out would make a statement he wasn't sure he actually wanted to make.

'I see,' she said slowly. 'In that case, we better make sure our stories are very straight indeed.' Willow still sat straight-backed and at attention, expression completely unread-able, but Logan sensed that she was panick-ing. He didn't blame her—living with the in-laws would be daunting even if this was a real marriage.

'Think of it more like a hotel with a per-manent crotchety guest you will run into now and then,' he reassured her. 'To balance it out, it's right on the ocean front with access to the beach, we have a pool and tennis courts, and Romney is a really nice town—great shops and cafes, with Boston within easy access.'

'It's okay. Just a surprise, that's all.' Willow attempted a smile, but her eyes were still troubled, and Logan felt a pang of guilt. Was this worth it? Worth the lies and the subterfuge, the upending of Willow's life? Should he have just come clean in the study? But he knew his father all too well, how unforgiving and harsh he could be. Willow would leave well recompensed. It was all going to be all right.

CHAPTER FOUR

THE FLIGHT WAS smooth enough, but Willow felt as twisted inside as if they were going through the worst turbulence.

What on *earth*? Logan might have mentioned they'd be sharing a house with his father earlier, especially as he was the person they had to completely convince of their marriage's veracity. Despite Logan's reassurances, she was sure this meant no let-up in the pretence from breakfast to supper, seven days a week. Could they really manage it? Could she?

Willow continued to quiz Logan on his college—Dartmouth—his major—environmental science—his favourite colour—blue—and food—impossible to choose. But as she asked question after question, she couldn't help but worry about what next day, week, month and year held in store. She had anticipated that the next week would be filled with moving into her new home and getting her bearings in both a strange city and a new life. Being confronted with her father-in-law straight off had not figured in her calculations, nor had living with the man whom they were trying to fool. Her stomach continued to twist and turn as she tried to quell the rising panic.

'Okay, that is more than enough about me,' Logan said finally. 'I'll set you a paper later to test your memory, but now it's your turn to answer twenty questions.'

'I attended university while I worked, so mostly day release and self study. My favourite colour is pale sea green, my go-to comfort meal is a really well-cooked baked potato with a lot of butter, I dislike rudeness and people who litter, and I prefer reading to television,' she answered promptly.

'That's five down. Have you always lived in London?'

Willow bit her lip, always uncomfortable when discussing her childhood. 'We travelled a lot,' she said.

'That can be rough. Your dad's job?'

'He didn't really have one job. He kind of flitted from project to project. My mother too.'

'Was it just you and—Skye, isn't it?'

'At first. I'm the eldest. Skye's just sixteen

months younger. Then Leaf came along a few years later, when I was twelve, Summer six years after that, and then Rainbow a year after Summer.' She couldn't help but laugh as she saw him take that in. 'My parents were inspired by the natural world.'

'They're all good, solid names.'

'Individually, maybe. As a group they're a bit much, but it could be worse. We knew one family who named all their children from Arthurian legend. Leaf always says at least he's not Galahad.'

'Good point. Do they all live in London as well?'

'Oh, no, my parents only stayed in London while I did my GCSEs and A levels, then they left Skye and me behind while they headed off with our other siblings on their next adventure. But they've been settled in Shetland for some time now. I think Leaf will stay there for good, and it's all the girls really know.' Recounting her upbringing just brought home how different their lives were, had been. 'Logan. How will we make this work? I'm not from your world. I'm not sophisticated…'

'Hey.' In a moment he was beside her, taking her hand in his. Despite her need for this to be a business relationship, nothing more,

Willow found her fingers curling around his, holding on tight. 'You're the one choosing exhibitions and operas for our imaginary dates. I'm just a surfer dude. Willow, if I had a moment's doubt that you couldn't handle this, I would never have suggested this arrangement. I wouldn't put you in that position. And if you have changed your mind, just say. I'll turn the plane around.'

For one glorious second, she imagined doing just that. It wasn't too late to back out. After all, her colleagues were still under the illusion that she was heading off on a secondment. She could just claim it had been cancelled. She'd given Skye the same story too; as she had told Logan, she hated lying to her, but her sister was such a romantic that she'd immediately try and twist what was—what had to be—a sensible, mutually convenient business arrangement into something rose-tinted and tinged with expectation. As far as Skye was concerned, Willow had been offered a huge pay rise for this year and had offered to use it to pay the rent on the cafe and apartment, taking over the agreement for her sister. Willow herself would never have bought the subterfuge, would have been filled with questions, needed to speak with the landlord herself, but Skye was much more easy-going. The family often joked that they were misnamed; Skye was pliant and bent with the wind, Willow the one who oversaw everything.

And it was for Skye—and Mia and Harper and Noah—that she was doing this. So no matter what other surprises lay in store, she had to be ready.

'Thank you. I really appreciate you saying that,' she said, reluctantly untangling her fingers from his. 'But no need. I'm ready.'

She had to be.

Getting off the plane, however, was unexpectedly difficult. Despite her earlier resolution, Willow wanted to hang on to the door like a child and demand to be taken home. But even with the necessary questions occasioned by Willow's brand-new spousal visa, immigration was surprisingly quick and smooth, and before she could really catch her breath, she was through the airport and in a limousine. Despite her nerves, she found herself looking about her curiously. As a child there had been no money for international travel despite the family's itinerant lifestyle. As an adult she hadn't indulged in more than a few city mini-breaks, treating herself to culture and history. Skye always joked that even in leisure, Willow had to keep busy, had to learn something.

But apart from her ill-fated trip to Vegas, she had never visited the States and soon found herself absorbed by the sights and sounds, her fatigue forgotten as the car purred across the city, then out onto a highway running alongside the coast. Everything was different from the road signs to the painted wooden houses glimpsed through the trees, the names on the highway a mix of the familiar and the new.

'Do you drive?' Logan interrupted her thoughts, and Willow reluctantly turned her attention back to him, all too conscious of his proximity. It had been easy to keep her distance in her apartment, on the plane, but now, here in the back of a car, she couldn't escape the scent of him, the heat that radiated off him. Her mouth dried. She couldn't deny that she was always aware of where he was, what he was doing, that every cell in her body remembered how he felt, how he tasted, how he touched, how he kissed.

She curled her hands into fists. She needed to remember how she behaved with him, how he brought out a side of her she had hoped didn't exist. She couldn't allow that side to show. She needed to end this year with her sister's future saved intact. That was the goal, not momentary pleasure.

Willow shifted slightly to one side until her arm brushed the door. 'I never learned,' she said at last. 'Living in London, there seemed no need.'

'I could teach you. The town is walkable from the house, and you can get a train to Boston, but as you probably know, the States are pretty car-dependent. You'll have more freedom if you drive.'

'Thank you, I appreciate that.' Appreciated it, but there was no way she was allowing herself to be trapped in the intimate surroundings of a car with him more than absolutely necessary. If she did need to learn to drive, she would find a professional to teach her.

Throughout their journey, Willow had glimpsed the ocean, blue and vast, through her window, but now the highway ran close to the coast, and she gasped at the beauty of the coastline as it came into view. It was a dune-filled coast with picturesque harbours and charming small towns clustered along it. Despite her apprehension and tiredness, excitement stirred. She'd moved around a lot as a child, but their destinations had been limited by where the narrow boat they lived on could travel and moor, and their adventures had never taken them to the sea. Willow let down the window and breathed deep, pine and salt and wildness filling her lungs.

'You grew up here?'

'Yes.'

'Lucky,' she breathed, turning to him. 'I always dreamed of living by the sea.'

'In some ways, I guess it was idyllic. I learned to sail and surf young. My cousin lived down the road. The beach was our playground. In others…' He shrugged. 'Hey. Nobody wants to hear a poor little rich boy whine about his childhood. Look, we're nearly there.'

As they turned off the highway into the pretty town, Logan pointed out local landmarks, the old stone church, the school he'd attended before being sent to a private prep school a few towns along, the Inn his uncle owned, where his mother had grown up, and myriad other details. It was clear he was proud of his home and eager to show it off— but Willow knew she was walking into a tense situation between father and son. The more Logan talked, the more she realised how little she was prepared for what awaited her at the end of her journey.

Logan's chest tightened as the high gates swung open and the car turned into the long, sweeping drive. Coming home had always had this effect on him, never knowing what his reception would be. He hoped for indifference, but far too often it was criticism and anger. Was he a fool subjecting himself to this day after day—and now not just him but Willow as well?

But no, he was a Hartwell, and this was his home. His grandfather made that very clear. And Hartwells didn't run away from their problems. He had done that for long enough.

'Here we are,' he said, hoping his voice betrayed nothing but his usual studied insouciance. 'Lookout House.'

'My goodness,' Willow breathed. 'I knew it was big but…this is insane, Logan!'

'It was called a cottage when it was built,' he told her, and her incredulous expression turned into a grin.

'Then you must be descended from Marie Antoinette, because you could fit twenty actual cottages in there and have room to spare.'

Like its counterparts south of Boston in Rhode Island, the Hartwell summer cottage had been modelled on fanciful fairy-tale chateau lines, with ornate stonework, gables galore, balconies and balustrades shading in terraces from every downstairs room, the whole positioned on a slope to take in the ocean views on three sides.

He slanted a glance at Willow, who sat stock-still, clearly taking in every detail. 'It's a palace,' she said after a while, disbelieving.

'That was the general idea. After a while, the Hartwells seemed to think they were royalty. Come on, let me show you around.'

Logan was both relieved and irritated that his father hadn't deigned to come out and meet them as he helped Willow out of the car and directed the driver to bring their cases in.

'Okay, I'll show you the gardens later. Let's start here.' He led her into the wide double-height hallway with its grand staircase that bisected the house, branching out into two galleries with corridors leading off.

Willow paused by a large polished dresser, reaching out to touch the smooth wooden surface.

'Eighteenth-century,' Logan told her. 'There's a similar one in the Metropolitan Museum.'

She snatched her hand back. 'I can't believe you grew up here.'

'Some areas are much more normal,' he reassured her, but Willow didn't look any more convinced as Logan gave her a quick tour of the main communal areas, her eyes growing wider as they traversed from one end of the ground floor to the other. 'And that,' Logan said as they passed the library door, 'is my father's lair. But we can save formal introductions until later when you've had a chance to freshen up.' After all, any real father-in-law meeting his son's wife for the first time would have come out to meet them, be waiting on the doorstep to welcome the new member of the family. But welcoming wasn't Logan Hartwell II's style.

He could see indecision plain on her face, until she shook her head. 'No, I think it's better to say hello straight away.'

Part of Logan was still conditioned to rap on the heavy oak door and wait for his father's bark bidding him enter, but he pushed the instinct away and opened the door. Usually he would have ushered Willow in before him, but protectiveness overrode chivalry and he went in first, waiting until she was by his side before strolling further into the long, high-ceilinged room, with its floor-to-ceiling book-lined shelves.

As usual, his father had the blinds semi-drawn, turning what should have been a light-filled space with stunning ocean views into a dark, intimidating space. The library was almost aggressively masculine, with dark leather chairs and sofas, the dark green paint and blinds reminiscent of a gentleman's club. It lacked only the cigar aroma. The man himself sat behind his huge desk. Logan took a long, deep breath to calm his anger when his father didn't get to his feet, merely sat back and waited in silence for them to approach him as if he really were a king on a throne.

'Willow, this is my dad, also confusingly called Logan. Dad, this is Willow Jones.' He deliberately sounded informal, confident.

'Jones?' His father raised his eyebrows. 'Not Hartwell?'

'We haven't decided that yet.' He ushered Willow into one of the chairs and sat next her, his smile bland. 'It's all been such a whirl-wind.'

'Yes, I'm confused about that part myself.' His father made no move to join them. 'Why the rush? The secrecy?'

'I always wanted to get married in Vegas.' Willow sounded cool and collected. Her faint smile showed no sign of intimidation. 'We knew that with the distance and such busy lives, organising a formal wedding would be difficult, and I thought a Vegas wedding would be romantic.' Her smile widened a little, as if she were recalling some wonderful memory. 'And it really was.'

Well, well, well. Willow Jones could play

the game. Not just play it, she was in an elite league. Logan reached over to take her hand, threading his fingers through hers. Her touch was cool, and yet his skin heated at the contact. 'It might seem like a rush, but we have been serious for quite some time. Willow didn't want the news we were dating to get out. She had her position to consider.'

His father leaned back even further, but Logan could tell by the tightening of his jaw that he wasn't as at ease as he affected to be. 'Ah, yes. Ms Jones's position. I have your résumé here.' Willow stiffened, and Logan tightened his grip to reassure her, but she was equal to the challenge.

'Call me Willow, please. After all, we're family now.'

Logan wanted to applaud. Instead he squeezed her fingers. 'And it's not a job interview, Dad.'

His father's jaw tightened further. 'No formal schooling until you were fifteen. Is that right?'

'My parents lived on a boat, so I was home-schooled.' Logan tried not to show his surprise. After all, a doting new husband should know these things. She'd mentioned travelling but neglected that pertinent detail. 'They took a permanent mooring in London near where

I live now so I could take my exams. As you can see, despite my unconventional upbringing, I got all A stars.'

'But you didn't go to college?'

'I turned down a place at Oxford to take a job which allowed me to study to be an accountant through work. It meant no debt and real-life experience. I qualified in half the usual time and then studied part-time, first for a business finance degree and then my MBA.'

Good God, she was magnificent. Brains, beauty and grit.

'Hmm, a distinction in your MBA, I see.'

'I started at Hartwell Corporation when I was twenty-five and have been promoted twice. I take my career very seriously, Mr Hartwell. That's why I was keen to keep my relationship with Logan under wraps. I want no allegations of favouritism or nepotism. I've worked hard to get where I am.'

His father's grunt wasn't unkind. 'It's a little too late for that. Once the world knows, rumours will fly. They usually do, but we don't have to pay them any heed.' His father adjusted his glasses, usually a sign he was thinking. 'It's an impressive résumé, and your colleagues speak very highly of you. Good strategic brain and a clear thinker. Truth is, we could do with a bright girl like you joining us at the top. The family has shrunk to just Logan and me. We need new blood, and you have the right skills.' His father sounded as smug as if he had arranged the match himself. 'You'll need to carry on proving yourself, of course, especially after such a secretive wedding, but it could be a lot worse.'

Willow was very still. Logan didn't blame her. Neither of them had expected what was, for his father, a fulsome welcome.

'Don't get carried away, Dad. You're embarrassing my wife,' Logan drawled, deliberately breaking the tension. 'It's been a long day, and I'm sure Willow will want to get settled in, so...'

'I've arranged for you to have your grandparents' rooms,' his father said abruptly, and Logan, on the verge of getting up, sat down heavily.

'Sorry?'

'Your rooms were fine for a single man, but not for a married couple. I had your things transferred. Feel free to redecorate any way you want,' he added to Willow. 'This is your home now.'

'Thank you.' Willow looked more than a little stunned. Logan was feeling pretty knocked out himself. His father might not have stood on the doorstep with welcome cookies, but he had been—for him—pretty conciliatory. Almost pleasant.

'Yes, thank you.' Logan wasn't entirely sure how he felt about the move. His grandparents' rooms had been a sanctuary throughout his childhood, the only part of the house where he had felt secure—and wanted. They were the first place he visited when returning from school, the last place he ran to before heading back. They were home—and now he would be sharing them with Willow.

But his own rooms were too small for two, and his plan to give Willow her own space might have raised eyebrows and set off the kind of rumours they wanted to avoid. This unexpected gift was probably the best solution. He stood and held his hand out to help Willow up. 'Let's go and explore our new home.'

It felt distinctly odd to head up the wide curving staircase which bisected the house, and instead of turning right to the side of the house where he had always slept, turn left. His grandparents had occupied the master suite, rooms on the first and second floor which incorporated the largest of the turrets with which the architect had adorned the house.

The suite was hidden behind a white door at the end of the gallery. He opened it and ushered Willow through to the wide hallway. It was exactly the same as when his grandparents had been alive with its polished wooden floors and seascapes on the white wall mirroring the views through the windows which lined the corridor. It opened out into a huge corner sitting room, views out to sea from two aspects. Willow went straight over to one of the windows, touching the wooden seat and blue cushions reverently. 'I always wanted a window seat.'

'Take your pick. There's plenty to go round.' He showed her the study which opened on one side of the sitting room and the small snug his grandparents had used as a TV room on the other before leading her back through the sitting room to the hallway.

The stairs were hidden behind a panelled door leading to the second floor. which was furnished with two good-sized bedrooms each with an en suite and dressing room. Then stairs spiralled up into the turret room. He gestured to Willow to head up. 'If you like window seats, I think you are going to approve of what's up there.'

She gave him a questioning look before ascending the stairs, her small cry as she reached the top the reaction he'd hoped for. 'Oh, my goodness,' Willow breathed as Logan joined her in the circular room. She moved from window to window, taking in the stunning three-sixty view. 'This is like something from a fairy tale.'

'It was my grandmother's sewing and reading room. Her sanctuary from the obligations of being married to the head of the Hartwell family,' Logan explained, resting his hand on the walnut sewing box still beside the rocking chair, despite the owner's death a decade before, grief momentarily flooring him. 'When she married my grandfather, he lived here with his brother and sister, parents and an uncle and aunt.' The house had been designed to be filled with people. It echoed with just two. 'She found it overwhelming at times. She always said being able to escape here saved their marriage.'

'What happened to them all?'

'My great-great-uncle and aunt lived here until they died, just before I was born. They didn't have children of their own. My great-uncle never married. He ended up moving to Sydney to manage the Australian office and died out there a few years ago. My great-aunt did marry. She had three daughters, so as you have probably worked out, my father exaggerates when he says there are no Hart-wells left, although my great-aunt changed her surname.'

'Are her family involved with HartCo?'

He shook his head. 'No, her daughters all married and settled far from here. My second cousins were raised in France, Seattle and California, respectively. They have lives away from Romney and HartCo and seem to like it that way.'

'So what happens if you don't have children, Logan?'

'I don't know,' he said honestly. 'We'd probably turn it into a public company, issue shares to all those cousins in the process.'

'Would that be a good thing?'

'You're the financial director. You tell me.'

She moved over to the window. 'From a financial point of view, it wouldn't necessarily be a bad thing. An injection of cash is always a bonus, and a more diverse board with real decision-making powers stands up to scrutiny better than one man reporting to a board he chairs and helped recruit. But it would overturn centuries of history.'

'Yes, it would.'

'So why are you wasting time with me? Don't you want to get married for real, have a family, ensure the succession?'

And that was the million-dollar question.

'One day,' he said slowly. 'I know it's my duty. But one step at a time.'

'Duty? What about love?'

'It's not been an issue so far.' He shrugged. 'Maybe I'm irredeemably unlovable.'

'Logan…' she said softly, and he swallowed, despising himself for letting his guard down. He barely knew this woman. What was he doing telling her things he barely admitted even to himself?

'Do you want this room?' He changed the subject abruptly. 'For your study, sanctuary, whatever you need?'

'Really?' Willow's smile lit up the whole room, and Logan's heart hitched.

'Every princess needs a tower to escape to.'

'I'm more the goose maid than the princess, but thank you. Yes, I'd love it.'

'Great, you can furnish it as you like. I'll make sure you get a credit card tomorrow. The one thing this family doesn't lack is money, so seriously, spend what you like.'

'I don't need your money.' She was straight-backed, eyes alight with fiery determination and pride. 'I still have my salary. There's no need…'

'There's every need. It's part of the deal. Besides, you'll need clothes.'

'I have clothes.'

'You have suits, and some casual clothes. They won't be enough. It might sound ridiculous, but you'll need the right labels to represent the family. There are bound to be fundraising galas, summer parties, all kinds of social invites ahead. People will want to meet the new Mrs Hartwell. You'll need to dress appropriately or questions will be asked.' He stopped then, suddenly appalled. Was this the conversation his father had had with his mother? A child of her time, she had loved the crocheted vests, long hippy skirts, and slip dresses of the era, all worn with her beloved big boots. 'Obviously you will wear whatever you're most comfortable in,' he amended. 'But whatever you've brought with you, you'll need triple at least, plus jewellery. Think of it as expenses allowing you to purchase the tools to do your job. Nothing more.'

'Okay. Got it.' But the excitement that had radiated from her when he had suggested she keep the turret room for her own had faded, and that was on him, suggesting she needed to be different. Were the Hartwell men destined to make the same mistakes with their brides, even when the marriage was a fake?

And did that mean Logan was no better than his father?

It wasn't something he wanted to dwell on, but as he continued to show Willow around the estate, he couldn't shake the realisation that marriage to him came with a price he hadn't reckoned on. But what did he expect? He was a Hartwell after all.

CHAPTER FIVE

To WILLOW'S SURPRISE, the next couple of weeks passed quickly and far more easily than she'd expected, especially when she thought of the scramble to get things together before her move. Logan—and his father—suggested she take a couple of weeks off to acclimatise to her new home before returning to work, and although routine was important to her, she appreciated the opportunity to know the area. She still wasn't entirely sure what her new role at HartCo entailed, but Logan's father was hinting at something at the executive level, a prospect that both excited and terrified her. She was here on false pretences, after all.

But for all the strangeness—and the tension that permeated the house whenever Logan and his father were together—she discovered that she liked her temporary home. She adored being able to access the beach whenever she wanted, taking herself for long daily walks by the ocean. The temperature was still fairly chilly, but spring teased the air, and she enjoyed having so much space to herself. She also liked the pretty town of Romney with its attractive wooden shops and houses and soon got into a routine of an early morning walk followed by a coffee from one of the three open-all-year-round cafes, often with some kind of delicious pastry or cake.

And she loved the house. Yes, it was ridiculously huge, and yes, it was absurdly ornate, but for all that she could tell, it was also a much-loved family home, which made the estrangement of the two current occupants even more of a shame. Every room had a view or a hidden nook for reading or an interesting feature. She especially loved the apartment she shared with Logan and her turret study. Some afternoons she threw open all the windows and wrapped herself in a blanket to perch on the window seat and try to read, but mostly gaze out on the view. It was strange, the feeling of contentment watching the ocean gave her. After all, she was living a temporary life with no idea what happened next, deviating from her carefully laid plans. The thought should—and did—make her stomach knot with anxiety. But somehow, when she stared out to sea, she felt like this was exactly where she was supposed to be.

To her relief, sharing with Logan was a lot less awkward than she had expected as well. With two en suite bathrooms and two dressing rooms, the housekeeper didn't seem to find it strange she kept her belongings in a different room to Logan's—or maybe she was too well paid to notice. Still, Willow made a point of mentioning that she sometimes moved through to the other room when she had trouble dropping off. She didn't want any gossip to reach Logan's father's ears and put her sister's lease at risk.

It was early days, but for now it all seemed to be working as Logan had planned.

That should have made things easier, but instead every day Willow grew more aware how little she knew the man with whom she had agreed to share a year. Gone was the laughing, confident man who had somehow made her want to be someone else entirely. Instead Logan seemed to wear a mask at all times, hiding any real emotion from her. He was calm and courteous and did his best to make her feel at home, but he kept himself completely apart both emotionally and physically. It was what she had wanted—it was what they had agreed—and yet she found herself somehow feeling lost and lonely, missing the camaraderie they had forged in Vegas, or even the ease they'd managed on the day they had travelled here. During the plane ride, she had thought they might forge some kind of friendship, but now they were barely acquaintances.

Logan wore a very different mask with his father: nonchalant and yet guarded, always ready with a quip, but not letting any real emotion through. It made the shared mealtimes exhausting, and Willow was always relieved to be able to plead jet lag at the end of the meal and creep up to her turret with a book. She read until late and then, exhausted, would crawl to her bed and try and sleep. But try as she might, she couldn't forget that just a wall separated her from Logan, and nor could she forget that night in Vegas.

Every sound reminded her of his proximity, reminded her of how it had felt to have him next to her, over her, under her... She had never felt like she had that night, never felt so wanted, so desirable, so free. It had been intoxicating and terrifying in equal measure, and knowing the man who had made her come alive was so close and yet so unreachable unsettled her to her core. It had been her decision to keep their relationship businesslike, the right decision, but with every day, it seemed that Logan was further away than ever.

It was going to be a long, lonely year.

It was a beautiful spring morning, the sun already beaming down turning the ocean silvery blue, when Willow got in from her usual walk. She'd resisted the pastries this morning, and so she headed to the smaller dining room off the kitchen where the Hartwells usually took breakfast. Their housekeeper, Brigid, lived out, and the men usually helped themselves to toast and cereal or the fruit salad she left prepared for them. Willow took her coffee into the dining room, ready for a light breakfast, only to halt in surprise when she saw Logan at the table, laptop open in front of him, a slice of toast in one hand.

With Nate still in Hawaii, Logan had double the work to do at the company they co-owned, and usually headed out to the Romney office and factory early, returning mid-afternoon to hole himself up in his study to take over his HartCo responsibilities. He looked exhausted, shadows darkening his blue eyes, a sign, she thought, of mental tiredness as well as physical. It wasn't that long since he had been in hospital. He really needed to take it easier.

'Hi,' she said, staying standing, not sure what to do and realising with a start just how little she actually saw of him. No wonder the first two weeks had been easier than she had expected. She felt like she'd been getting to know a new and usually absent flatmate, not adjusting to marriage.

Because it *was* a marriage, legal and above board, if slightly unusual in origin. For all she felt she was playing a part, it was easier, better for her to remember that it was real. That way she was less likely to slip up.

'Hi.' He eyed her travel mug. 'Where are you getting your coffee from?'

'I vary my custom across all three cafes, but today I went to the Surf Shack. It was almost nice enough to sit on a bench outside and drink it there.'

'Spring has definitely sprung,' he agreed. 'And good choice. I think their coffee is the best, not that I'd say that anywhere near my uncle. He prides himself on his coffee.'

'The Inn is the one place I haven't tried yet, but of course they're not open at breakfast.' She paused, uncertain how to continue, although surely conversation should flow easily between husband and wife. 'If I'd known you were at home, I would have brought you one, but you're usually gone so early...'

Logan rubbed a hand over his face. 'I'm sorry, I know I've neglected you…'

'I don't need babysitting, Logan. But as you are here, it's a good time to discuss what happens next.'

'Next?'

'Work-wise for me.' She paused and searched for the right words. 'I have really enjoyed having two weeks off. I think I needed it, to be honest, but it's time for me to get back to work. I don't know if anything has been said to my colleagues yet, but if not, then we need to think of the best way to tell them about us. I don't want to keep misleading people I've worked with for several years, especially as the truth will leak out sooner rather than later, and I would prefer for them to hear the news from me. Plus,' she added, 'I want to work from the Boston office a couple of days a week, not hide myself here. I don't have to go in with your father. I'll be fine on the train.' That was an understatement. She really didn't want to spend an hour twice a day in a close confined space with Logan's father, who was driven to the city four days a week, usually leaving at seven, returning sometime around six.

'Ready to spring at them. That's the spirit.' Willow hadn't expected Logan's father to still be at the house either, startled as he walked into the room, as casual as she had ever seen him in a smart polo shirt and freshly ironed navy trousers.

'Good morning, sir,' she said.

'No need for that, girl. Call me Logan.'

Willow only smiled noncommittally. There was no way she would ever get used to calling the two men by the same name. If this marriage didn't have an end date and they had children, would there be an expectation of a Logan Prestwood Hartwell IV? And would she have been able to insist on a second Willow? Not that she wanted to. Willow had vowed long ago that any children of hers would be given the most inconspicuous of names. Willow and Skye were innocuous enough on their own, but add in her siblings and the family had roused more than their fair share of attention—and mockery.

'So, you're ready for the office, eh?' Logan's dad pulled out a chair and sat down, barely acknowledging his son. 'That's good. I'd like to take you in myself, introduce you around. I've ordered an office on the top floor to be prepared for you. We can chat about what we want you to do when you start officially, but I can tell you, Willow, we're excited to have you on the leadership team.'

The *what*? Willow had been aware that

some kind of nepotistic promotion was coming her way and had spent the last two weeks reminding herself that it was only for a year and to look upon the opportunity as valuable work experience, but this meant being catapulted straight into the highest echelon of the company. She was sure she wasn't ready— and knew full well this wasn't a deserved elevation. If she wasn't Logan's wife, there was no way she would have been considered for the leadership team, let alone whilst still in her twenties – if only just!

'Welcome to the HartCo top floor.' Logan's smile was reassuring, and she sensed he knew exactly what she was feeling. 'I've recently started there as global head of operations, you already know Dad, and you'll find the others very down-to-earth considering their elevated positions. Nadia is British like you. She was the European CEO before Dad persuaded her to move over here and take on a global role. I think you'll like Finn. He was editor-in-chief of *our Boston newspaper*. We all report to the board, apart from Dad, who heads up both.'

Willow knew the names, of course, but she had never addressed as much as a word to them before, and now she would be on the same level. 'It just seems so sudden.'

'Nonsense.' Logan's father dismissed her

concerns with a wave of his hand. 'From what I've heard, it's well deserved. At least you know HartCo inside out, unlike this son of mine.'

Logan ignored the dig with a grace Willow guessed was born of long practice.

'But Logan was born to it. It's in his blood,' she said, forcing an innocuous smile. 'Add in the fact he's grown his own business from the ground up and he's probably the biggest asset you have, able to bring in fresh ideas whilst knowing the importance of tradition.'

Logan's father didn't reply, but the look he gave her was a shrewd one. Logan simply went on eating his toast as if he wasn't the subject under discussion, but when his father wasn't looking, he winked at Willow. 'Remind me to get some of that coffee,' was all he said.

'I'm golfing today.' Logan's dad got to his feet and picked up the newspaper that was always delivered straight off the press, arriving on the porch in the early hours. He would have read the digital edition whilst on his exercise bike, but liked to see the day's paper in print as well. 'I'll take you in tomorrow, Willow. See you down here at seven.' And with that he was gone. The air in the room instantly lightened.

'Logan.' Willow kept her voice low in case

her father-in-law was close by, but she couldn't not say anything. 'Skipping several rungs of the ladder wasn't our agreement. It isn't right. I'm not qualified. Not yet.' But for all the uncomfortable twisting in her stomach at the thought of being found out as a fraud receiving an unearned promotion, Willow was aware of a tinge of excitement. She was ambitious and capable and, temporarily at least, she was part of the family who owned HartCo. True, thousands of jobs depended on the decisions made by those at the top, but each region and division of the venerable media company, from publishers to newspapers to the social media divisions working with Silicon Valley start-ups, had a full management structure. It wasn't as if she would be single-handedly responsible for the financial viability of every project or company under the HartCo brand.

She couldn't deny that despite her concerns, she wanted this.

'Actually, for what it's worth, I think it's more than right,' Logan's smile was reassuring. 'You'll be a great addition to the leadership team, Willow. I've seen your work and spoken to your colleagues. Yes, you probably could have done with more than a few months at the regional director level first, maybe a couple of years in a different region, but this is where you were heading anyway.'

'Really?' She wasn't sure why, but she trusted him to be honest with her, even if they were engaged in a deception with everyone else.

'Really. Embrace it, Willow. You deserve it. And talking of deserving, I know I've neglected you shamelessly since we arrived...'

'Oh, no, it's fine. I've enjoyed finding my way around.'

'But—' he ignored her automatic interjection '—I mean to remedy that today. You need some outfits worthy of the top floor, and you deserve a celebratory lunch. How does a day in Boston sound?'

'You can afford to take the time off?'

His mouth twisted into a wry smile. 'Barely, but I can manage. I think we both could do with a day out.'

'Thank you. That will be lovely.'

As she ran upstairs to change, Willow told herself her excitement was due to spending a day in the city at last, but she was too self-aware not to know that the prospect of spending it with Logan was more than half the attraction. True, she was more than a little scared of the person she was with him, the person he made her want to be, the attraction that hummed through her veins whenever he was near, but at the same time she couldn't deny that she craved it too. Surely a little time alone with him wouldn't do her any harm?

Of course, she had used that logic in Vegas, and that was why she was here, new life, new role, and none of it really hers. She needed to be careful to remember that. To keep a barrier up at all times, no matter how much Logan tempted her to lower it.

Logan had suggested they go by train to give her a chance to experience the commute. 'So you're not dependent on my father if I'm not travelling in,' he said, and Willow found herself transfixed by the scenery as it flew past. She felt more like a tourist than ever, not a woman who would soon be commuting on this line. The holiday feeling continued as they disembarked from the train and Logan explained the metro system to her and the best way to get to HartCo's imposing offices, recently moved to the Seaport area after over two hundred years in the centre of the distinguished old city.

Willow looked around her with a shiver of pleasure. Boston was busy, as busy as London, as busy as Vegas in some ways, but the feel of the city was completely new. Much smaller than London, much less flashy than

Vegas, she found herself drawn to it, just as she was drawn to the canal near her flat and the cottages which lined it. It felt right, like it fitted her.

'I don't want to go shopping. Can we just sightsee?' she asked, and Logan laughed.

'I don't want to resort to stereotypes about women and shopping…'

'Then don't.'

He held his hands up in mock surrender. 'I'm just saying that you have a credit card with no limit, and I am about to take you to one of the country's best shopping streets. Most people, man or woman, would be ready to blaze a red-hot trail through those shops.'

'I'm not most people.'

He squeezed her hand. 'That is very true.' It was the briefest, the lightest of caresses, but it shot through her like lightning, setting every nerve aflame. 'But you do need some clothes. Come on. For every outfit you buy, I'll owe you an hour's sightseeing.'

'Deal.' That was a bargain she was more than happy to make.

Their first stop was Back Bay, where Logan introduced her to Newbury Street and Boylston Street, which, he told her with a smug grin, fulfilled both the sightseeing and shopping agenda. She couldn't help but agree, delighted by the old red brick terraces which housed charming boutiques and high-end chains. Despite her reluctance, Willow found a couple of understated boutiques where she was persuaded to ditch her beloved neutral matching trouser suits for smart trousers in bright colours and modern cuts, dresses and jackets, mixing up pattern and texture in a way that was new to her. She soon added a few pretty dresses and some jeans, skirts and tops, finishing off her spree with a couple of formal gowns that, although she wouldn't admit it to Logan, took her breath away.

'That's—' she quickly counted up the boxes and bags Logan had arranged to be delivered '—sixteen hours you owe me.'

'My wish is your command. Hungry?'

The morning coffee and snatched slice of toast in the kitchen felt a long way away. 'Absolutely.'

'Then let's start with one of the Boston's best features, its culinary heritage and...' He flashed her a boyish smile. 'Tea is most definitely not on the menu.'

CHAPTER SIX

LOGAN HAD TOLD himself to keep his distance, emotionally and physically, from Willow. After all, he was to blame for her current predicament. True, in many ways she was getting as much as she gave, more even. In a year's time, her sister would be the owner of a valuable building in an up-and-coming part of London, and Willow herself had been given a huge boost up the career ladder. He had no doubt she'd excel at the top, and wherever her future was, she'd continue to fly. If they handled the news of the divorce right, she could probably stay on at HartCo too, especially if she made the impression he thought she might. But at the same time, he could see how she was struggling with her situation and knew she needed support. Willow Jones didn't want a penny she hadn't earned fairly, and she missed her sister terribly. She'd already sent several packages full of treats for her nieces and nephew back to London. There was no doubt that being parted from them was a huge wrench.

He also knew she had been totting up the value of the clothes she'd bought and wouldn't be surprised if she insisted on paying off the credit card with her own money. She had no interest in being anyone's trophy or corporate wife, and she would be uncomfortable being thrust into the limelight—but once she started work and attending functions with Logan and his family, there would be no hiding. The clothes he'd helped her buy were armour. She'd see that soon enough.

But for all he needed to support her, he couldn't deny that the attraction that had got them into this situation was all too alive and well. Logan was hyperaware of Willow whenever she was close by. She played down her looks and figure, her clothes could only be described as sensible, her make-up minimal, her hair usually pulled back, but to him that only enhanced her beauty. Her skin glowed, her hazel eyes were alight with curiosity and intelligence, and her full mouth needed no colour. His eyes were drawn to it whenever he let his guard down. She moved with fluidity and grace, transcending her forgettable clothes.

Although when she had left the dressing room, shy but glowing in a full-length fitted sheath in a matt gold that had brought out the natural lowlights in her hair and the amber in her eyes, his breath had literally been knocked from his body...

But despite the passion that had burned between them in Vegas, she had asked for a business relationship, and that meant no dwelling on her mouth or fixating on the hollow of her neck. It meant business and cheerful friendliness. No pushing beyond friendship even as she let her guard down, looking around her with eager curiosity, the reserve that kept him at bay swept away.

Their first stop was a famous Boston chain for Willow's first encounter with the renowned local clam chowder. She'd been doubtful at first as Logan instructed her to scatter her oyster crackers into the creamy broth, but one taste and she was lost.

'Why hasn't this been imported to the UK?' she asked as she contemplated her empty bowl with sad eyes, having scraped every last drop from it.

'Nowhere makes chowder like New England,' Logan said proudly. 'In fact, I'd say the Massachusetts shore is the only place you get the authentic taste.'

Chowder was followed by a visit to Quincy Market and the myriad food stalls, where they spent far longer than they intended choosing between all the sweet treats on offer. Ice creams in hand, they then strolled over the park to the narrow, winding cobbled streets of Beacon Hill.

'This is where the great and good used to live,' Logan told her. 'Many still do. These houses are prime real estate and very much sought-after. And this is the ancestral home, from where the Hartwells reigned Boston before they left the city.'

Willow stared up at the double-fronted house red-bricked house, with its shuttered windows, white steps leading up to the recessed front door, a lamp hanging down to illuminate it, just as it must have done three hundred years ago.

'It's got an air of grandeur,' she decided finally. 'But I think I like Lookout House better.'

'I'd rather live by the ocean.' Logan agreed. 'This is quaint but might get a little claustrophobic after a while.'

Offered a choice of tourist activities, Willow was clearly tempted by the aquarium, especially after Logan mentioned the vast penguin house at the centre of the building, but the sun was out and the air the warmest it had been since she arrived. Instead she decided to follow the Freedom Trail from Boston Common all the way to Little Italy, where they stopped for a glass of wine in one of the many trattorias, taking his teasing about the Revolution and the Boston Tea Party in good humour. 'It seems like a waste of good tea,' was all she commented as he filled her in on this particular part of Anglo-US relations.

'You know, I don't think I've ever been a tourist in Boston before,' Logan said, taking an appreciative sip of the nicely chilled wine. 'It's fun. And I don't come to this area enough. I vote we stay until we're hungry enough to eat here.'

'It really does feel Italian,' Willow agreed, eyeing up the huge pizzas being slung into the pizza oven opposite. 'I could almost be in Rome. I loved it there. I always meant to see more of Italy.'

'Have you travelled much?' The walk had done them both good, Logan decided, knocking off the edge of restraint that had still constrained them. It had been hard at first, not to think back to the last time he'd shown her around a city, to suggest sedate normal sightseeing rather than see how far he could push her to try new things. Getting Willow Jones to unwind had been one of the most satisfying days of his life. If only he hadn't gone too far…

But at the same time, he surprisingly didn't regret the outcome, even though they had ended up at this point, although he did feel for Willow, caught in the middle of the coldness that never seemed to thaw between his father and him. He liked Willow, enjoyed her company, liked having a third person in the house. It was just remembering that she wasn't really his that caught him out sometimes. He didn't love her, he barely knew her in many ways, but she seemed to be on his side, and that was too rare a thing.

'Only a little. I mean, obviously we travelled all the time as children, but only as far as a canal could take us, so we were a little restricted, and it was strictly UK only.'

'But living on a boat sounds like an adventure.'

Anything less like the stuffy environs of Lookout House was hard to imagine.

'That's one word for it. Narrow boat living is a lot more common now as house prices are so expensive, although there are permanent moorings in London that aren't much cheaper than renting a house, but when we were kids, it was definitively an unusual lifestyle. And we were more unusual than most. Families often choose a mooring and stay put during term time at least, but we never stayed in one place for too long.'

'Was it cramped?'

'Everything definitely had to be in its place. Have you ever been on a narrow boat?'

He shook his head. 'I'm more of an ocean sailor.'

'They're very different. They aren't built for speed, that's for sure, but they are ingeniously designed. We had a wood-burning stove before they were trendy, solar panels, and a rooftop garden. It was cosy in many ways, although there were times when I longed for my own space.'

He thought back to her modern apartment in a sterile building, her lack of clutter, of anything personal. It was light, airy, the opposite of cosy. 'You weren't tempted to keep living on one yourself?'

She shook her head emphatically. 'Not at all. Skye might have if they hadn't found premises for the cafe that included a flat. She was always much more comfortable than I was with our way of life, but as I got older, I yearned to stay in one place. London was the place that felt most like home, the place we returned to most. Maybe that's why I ended up living there. Plus it was London where we did get a permanent mooring for a few years so Skye and I could go to school close to where we live now. It was as if once the boat stopped, we got off and we never left.' She looked into the distance for a moment, lost in thought.

'You like living there?' He'd liked the little he'd seen of her neighbourhood. It had an authentic feel to it, still in the process of gentrification, but it was a long way from HartCo's trendy South Bank London offices, and the theatres and museums he knew she enjoyed.

'I do. It's home. In some ways it always was. It sounds silly...' She stopped and flushed.

'What does?'

'It's just, there are some cottages lining the canal. I can see them from my apartment window. They're really pretty, all painted different colours with gardens in front. I remember being about five and sailing past and seeing a couple of girls Skye's and my age playing tea parties in one of the gardens. They stopped and stared at us, we stared at them until we were past, and all I wanted was to be that girl in that garden.' She smiled at him. 'I have no idea why. It just looked like something from a book, a teddy bears' picnic in your own front garden. A garden you saw every day. A front door. The same view. That to me was as exotic as living on a canal boat was to those girls. Maybe that's why I settled in that area, that and because Skye was nearby, of course.'

'Maybe one day you'll own that cottage.' He was joking, but she nodded, completely serious.

'That's the plan. If I hadn't come here, I was thinking of selling the flat and buying one.'

'I'm sorry your plans didn't work out.'

'They will. It's just a short delay and, well, I'm ahead of schedule anyway.'

Now he was intrigued. She'd hinted at her schedule in Vegas. Mentioned a life plan. For someone whose ultimate life had been mapped out from the day he was born, the idea of setting goals for himself and ticking them off was completely alien.

And nothing about that day in Vegas had correlated with her list. That had obviously been part of its charm for her.

'Ah, yes, your to-do list. Tell me, is it an actual list? Do you keep it under lock and key?'

'In parchment written in blood?' She laughed, soft and musical, and Logan's chest clenched at the sound. He loved to hear her laugh. He got the sense that true, uninhibited laughing wasn't something she did often. This year, he would make her laugh as much as possible, he vowed.

'No, it's a mental list. Writing it down felt a little too solemn, you know, like the beginning of a film, not real life.'

'What's on it?'

She flushed then. 'It's all going to sound rather dull to someone who has won sailing championships and started his own multimillion-dollar business at fifteen.'

'Not at all. I had no plan. Things just happened and I went with them.' He was downplaying what he and Nate had achieved, he knew, but he was intrigued, and didn't want to put Willow off. 'That's why I'm so intrigued by your plans.'

'Really? Well, stop me if you find yourself nodding off.' She took a sip of her wine and pushed her hair off her face. 'Okay, the first thing was A levels. My parents were both university dropouts, and I was home-educated until my mid teens. They were very much of the learn-what-you-feel school of education. But I knew that if I wanted stability and a regular income, I needed qualifications.'

'You have what? Accountancy qualifications, a degree and an MBA? I'd say you were pretty well qualified.' And she'd been working whilst studying. It was impressive, laudable, but when had she taken time to have fun? To grow up as a person, as a woman, not just as a worker. Fun, something else to add to his now growing list for their year ahead.

This list-making was obviously catching.

'Then I wanted to own my own home, first a flat and then…' Her colour heightened. 'One of the cottages I mentioned. Ideally I want to be mortgage-free by forty.'

She could have been, if she'd accepted his postnuptial offer. Instead she'd put her sister's needs first. 'Sensible.'

'Having a place of my own is important. I guess you don't need to be a psychologist to figure out why. Then career-wise, I wanted to make it to director level.'

'Another tick.'

'And more than five years earlier than planned.' There was a hint of triumph in her smile. 'I'm so glad I made that jump on my own, grateful as I am for the opportunity your father has given me.'

'What else, outside work and study?' What else made her tick?

'Travel. I've been to about ten European capitals now. I'd like to visit them all.'

'Guidebook and tick list in hand?'

'Guilty as charged.'

'Marriage, kids?'

She hesitated, taking a sip of her wine. 'I'd like to get married one day, for real I mean, but I want to be established first. Independent. My parents married when they were nineteen, Skye when she was twenty. That's not for me.'

'That's young,' he agreed.

'Both couples are still together. But there has been so much instability. I mean, Skye nearly lost the house and business, and she has three children relying on her. Don't get me wrong, I love my Mia, Harper and Noah with all my heart. I am so glad they are in my life. And they are completely loved and well brought up, but there are times when I have had to step in to pay the bills, and I provide the treats. I'm happy to do so, always, it's just…' She bit her lip. 'Mum and Skye would say that love is the most important thing, that everything works out for the best. But someone has to *make* things work out.'

Logan studied her. No wonder she had agreed to this year, to securing her nieces' and nephew's future. 'And that person is you?'

'Like I said, I'm happy to do it. And now they will have the building, they'll be rent-free, it will all be different. Thank you for making that possible.'

'You drove the bargain, it's your doing. How about your parents? They're still together? Nineteen *is* really young.'

'It is—and they were. Young I mean, in every way. Mum always says she grew up alongside Skye and me, and that's true. In many ways they were—are—like older siblings. And that could be fun, but there are times when I felt as if I was the grown-up. They were always taking off on a whim or coming up with hare-brained schemes. Once they decided to run a travelling theatre. That was the craziest thing they tried. More than once they'd end up owing money, and we would sail off at night to avoid paying, or create some elaborate story as to how they'd pay. They weren't dishonest, just hopelessly naive. For one year they decided to go back to nature, and we moored up at a smallholding. That was the longest we stayed in one place until they brought us to London for my education. Neither of them knew the slightest thing about living off the land then.' She took another sip. 'Luckily they seem to be doing better with the croft, and they both have found other jobs up in Orkney too, so not reliant on just one thing. They are the kindest, most well-meaning people I know, but they live in this dream world. By ten I was managing the household finances, making sure we had money for fuel, for food.'

'It was that bad?' They couldn't have had

more different childhoods. His financially so secure he could have anything he wanted, secure in every way apart from his father's love. Whereas Willow had evidently been loved, but had been left wanting in other, crucial ways. No wonder she had a list. No wonder security was more important than adventure. No wonder that day in Vegas had been so against type.

'Bad? No. Not bad. I mean, often we were in second-hand clothes or homemade ones, but that was very much their ethos. They dropped out of education to try and live a more sustainable life, an alternative one. My mother was a first-year medical student, my dad the younger son of a very respectable family—they are all bankers and lawyers, public schools and top universities, you know the types. They were appalled when he used his trust fund to buy the boat. Dinner was sometimes potatoes and beans several nights in a row, but other times if whatever scheme they had concocted did well, we had plenty of money. They just didn't think about looking ahead to the less plentiful times. That was down to me. If I have children, I want to make sure they never have to think about how the bills are paid or worry that we're going to be chased for a bad debt. I want them to grow up in blissful ignorance of any of that. And if waiting means it never happens for me, that's a chance I am willing to take. I'll just carry on being the best aunt I can be.'

She finished the rest of her wine, her gaze faraway, eyes dark with memories, and Logan realised how little he knew his wife—but how much he enjoyed finding out about her. With every revelation, every confidence, he admired her more. Wanted her more.

But it was clear how much she deserved someone better than him. She deserved a man with no demons, a man who was worthy of love, a man who knew how to love, not a poor little rich boy who substituted adrenaline for affection, whose own father wished he was anybody else.

Sitting here, drinking wine, it was easy to imagine another life, one where they were really together, where they were a real married couple having an evening out. And even though Logan knew he was too old to play 'let's pretend,' there was a comfort in sinking into that deception. For this evening at least.

CHAPTER SEVEN

THE DAYS SOON settled into a pattern. After their day in Boston, Willow felt more comfortable with Logan, although she still couldn't believe she had told him so much about her childhood, about her dreams. But somehow she knew her confidences were safe with him. He respected her boundaries, making no move to persuade her to make their marriage physical, although she often saw the flare of appreciation in his eyes when he glanced her way, and would remember with a quiver just how his skin had felt against hers, the taste and feel of his mouth, the way he had set her alight, set her free. For one night only.

Lying in her bed, she couldn't help but think about Logan sleeping just next door. To imagine opening the door that divided them, sliding in between his sheets, winding around him. Sometimes the ache of longing was almost overwhelming, but she stayed firm. She had given into impulse with Logan Hartwell before, and her whole life had been upended. If one day could have such drastic consequences, then how would spending a prolonged period giving into her desires end? There was no good outcome, she knew that.

Besides, although she knew Logan wanted her, she also was aware how much he hid from her and the rest of the world. He either ignored his father's jibes or laughed them off. He never complained about the long days juggling two important roles or moaned about missing out on the sport she knew he loved, although he'd not been near a boat or on a board since his accident. He also barely mentioned Nate, although she was aware his cousin had recently had the first of several operations on his leg and was back in Romney recuperating. She had yet to meet any of his mother's family or Logan's friends, although their marriage was now common knowledge.

It was all a much-needed reminder that none of this was real or permanent and she had to safeguard her heart. And that meant safeguarding her body, no matter how tempted she was.

Luckily she was an old hand at resisting temptation. All those evenings when colleagues had headed out and she had gone home to study, things not bought so she could save, sunny weekends ignored in favour of work.

Willow had got into the habit of heading into the city most days. She rose early for a quick run on the beach before either taking the car in with Logan's father or, her preference, taking the train with other early commuters. She liked the routine of standing at the same spot on the platform coffee in hand, a nod of acknowledgement to other commuters. She tried to work on the way in, read on the way back, but mostly she sat and gazed out at the view. To her relief, she found her work challenging but interesting and soon realised that she was not just capable of fulfilling the role, but that she was adding value to the company. If anyone did feel she was in her position because of nepotism, they kept their feelings to themselves, and she found herself laughing at the good-natured teasing from colleagues in London over her surprise marriage and promotion, aware of a sting of regret that she hadn't got to know them better when she did work with them.

Logan also worked in Boston a couple of days a week, and on those evenings they often ate out, sometimes returning to Little Italy or heading to Chinatown or little Back Bay bistros. Other times they just hung out at Faneuil Hall or Quincy Market, grazing the food courts. The evenings were always enjoyable, and Logan was good company, but they hadn't returned to the intimate conversation of the first night out. She knew he was keeping himself closed off from her. Nor had they ventured out in Romney itself, and now that she'd been in the States for almost two months, Willow knew it was time they were seen together in Logan's hometown.

She spent the day working in her turret room, and it was well into the evening before she descended, unaccountably shy as she searched out Logan. It was one thing to fall into the habit of going out for drinks, quite another to extend an invitation to him. Doing so felt a little like asking him on a date.

But then again, they *were* married, she reminded herself. People expected to see them out together.

Logan had commandeered the study off their sitting room for the rare occasions he worked from home, although he usually worked from the Lona headquarters somewhere on the other side of town. Willow still hadn't visited his other business. He hadn't suggested it, and she was too shy to invite herself into such an important and personal part of his life, but she was intrigued. She'd done some research into Lona and discovered that it was a bona fide success story, its handmade boards sought after, its extensive range of accessories sold all over the world. Impressive for a summer project started by two surf-mad teenage boys.

'Hey,' she said after knocking on the partly opened door. She hadn't been in the study since moving in, but it looked no different to how it had looked during her first tour of their rooms almost two months earlier. Neither of them had made a start on the proposed renovations to their rooms. Willow didn't feel it was really her place to make any changes, knowing she wouldn't be here long enough to see them through, and Logan hadn't mentioned it. As his grandparents had furnished the rooms with solid, comfortable and tasteful antiques and in the soft greens, deep blues and matt whites Willow would probably have chosen, she felt at home anyway, more so than in the formal communal sitting rooms and spaces in the rest of the house. Logan sat at a handsome mid-century teak desk by the window. Built-in bookshelves filled the alcoves next to the chimney breast, and an inviting-looking leather armchair took up one corner.

The only new items were Logan's office chair and his laptop and monitor.

He looked up and smiled, and despite all her good intentions, her libido immediately sat up and begged for attention. 'Hey yourself. Good day?'

'Not bad, but too many long meetings for a Friday. I'm in need of some fresh air, and I fancy a walk on the beach.'

She hesitated. *Come on, Willow*, she admonished herself, *what's the worst that can happen?*

'Want to join me? I thought it might be nice to grab dinner afterwards. I still haven't been to your uncle's Inn, and someone was saying that his seafood platter was unmissable.'

She was aware of the plea in her voice and mentally kicked herself. *Don't be so needy.*

'If you don't have any other plans, of course.'

'No, none. A walk sounds nice. It's just…' He hesitated.

'Just what?'

Logan pushed his chair back and swivelled round to fully face her. 'I haven't been to the Inn since Nate's accident.'

'You've been busy,' she pointed out, and he nodded.

'I know, but he's been back for a few days now.'

'You've spoken to him though?' She knew

he had. That he spoke to his cousin daily, messaged him much more. What was going on here?

'Regularly. We're in touch. It's just...' He trailed off and looked away.

She could leave it. It wasn't her place to pry—but if she didn't, who would? Something was clearly bothering him. 'Just what?'

'The last time I actually saw him, he was in hospital with his leg in a cage, facing up to the knowledge that he had several operations and a hell of a lot of painful work ahead to get anywhere near to where he was. And even with all that, he may never be able to surf again, or climb or be as active as he once was.'

Willow ached at the studied calm in his voice, at odds with the torrent of emotions swirling in his navy eyes. How had she not realised how much guilt Logan was carrying? She sought to hide her sympathy, to sound as matter-of-fact as he was trying to be. 'It seems tough, I know, but he will get back much more mobility than they first feared, won't he? I know there was some concern over his spine, but they ruled out any permanent problems early on? Nate will walk and swim and boat, and who knows about the rest? Modern medicine can work miracles. It'll just take some time.'

Logan didn't reply for a long time, and when he did, he was almost inaudible. 'But not like he used to. It's one thing talking to him on the phone and messaging him, but to see him back at home, still needing crutches, in pain, knowing it's my fault. I know I'm a coward, but I haven't been able to face it.' He stared down at his hands. 'Dad's right. I'm bad luck.'

Willow searched for the right words. All along, this had been bubbling away underneath his calm, rather insouciant manner, and she hadn't had a clue. What else did he keep hidden? It occurred to her that it must be rather lonely being Logan Prestwood Hartwell III. 'It was an accident, Logan. Bad luck, yes, but no one's fault.'

'I was distracted, and that makes it my fault. I know that, Nate knows that, and his parents do too. I can pay for the health care and I can pay for the physio and I can make sure he has no work pressure, but I still can't turn back time. I can't put it right.'

'And that's why you're killing yourself doing two full-time jobs? Oh, Logan.' Her heart ached with sympathy.

'I should have gone to see him the day he returned rather than hiding behind work, should have been to see my uncle when he got back from Hawaii, and taken my punishment then. Just as I should have told Dad the truth about us straight away rather than pulling you into this mess of a family. I'm a coward, Willow, and that's the truth. But I guess I can't hide here forever.' He laughed, a twisted cynical sound that struck her like a blow. 'Maybe dinner at the Inn is a good idea. They won't throw me out if you're with me.'

'You were protecting me as well as yourself when you lied to your father,' she reminded him softly. 'I haven't forgotten that, even if you have. And I chose to come here, to live here as your wife, which is why I want to meet your uncle and aunt, and I want to meet Nate. Anyone who is so important to you is important to me. We may not live in the most conventional way, Logan, and we may know our end point, but this is still a marriage, sanctified by 'Elvis' himself, and that means I'm on your team.'

'There's no one else I'd rather have,' he said a little hoarsely, and their gazes caught and held.

'Right back at you.'

The air stilled. Willow was acutely aware of every detail from the small blond hairs on Logan's forearms to the stubble on his firm chin, the vee of chest exposed by the unbuttoned shirt at his throat, the way his eyes darkened almost to black. She licked her lips nervously and felt his attention shoot to her mouth, her whole body tingling as it did so.

'I'd better get ready...' she managed, but she couldn't move, held against the door frame by the power of his gaze alone.

'Yes...' he said, but he didn't break the connection between them. 'Willow...' It wasn't a question.

'Yes.' It was an acknowledgement of whatever strange undercurrent was swirling between them, the same tidal recognition and attraction that had swept them away in Vegas and deposited them here on this shore. She knew that she only needed to take one step and it would break over them. Willow didn't step out of line. She created the line. But how she wanted to.

And he would wait for her to make the first move, she knew that. His guilt over the accident, over the upending of her life ensured that. It was a first move part of her—an increasingly persistent part—really wanted to make.

'Right, see you in five.' Somehow she dragged herself off the door frame and took that step—only back, not forwards—and with that, the spell was broken.

'Absolutely.' Only a wry twitch of his mouth acknowledged that the moment had ever been.

Willow made it into her bedroom on shaky legs, heading straight to her dressing room, sinking onto the comfortable chaise in the corner, covering her face with her hands as she took several fortifying breaths.

He calls himself a coward, but at least he goes out and lives life. What do I do? Plan and tick off task after task, too afraid of consequences to offer comfort and be comforted. That was all that was, comfort. We are here together, holding on to this secret together. It makes sense there's a connection between us.

But it's more than that, she argued back against herself. *There was no secret, no forced proximity last time. We were strangers then. Look at the consequences!*

Your sister's livelihood saved? A boost to the top of the career ladder? A gorgeous oceanside home? An even more gorgeous husband who you know full well would be up for making this marriage a real one if you weren't so scared...

A real one with an end date. It's still a sham even if we were sleeping together.

What's a sham? You like each other. It's mutually beneficial. You said it yourself, you're on his side.

'Argh!' she exclaimed, exhausted by her own inner argument. She'd always had an impulsive side. How could she not with parents like hers? But she'd learned early to keep it contained and under control. Since meeting Logan, the urge to let that side of her run free was sometimes overwhelming.

But there was a reason she kept it locked away. The consequences of just living as her mood dictated were ones she knew all too well. That life led to uncertainty, to hardship, to bills unpaid and late-night flits.

It led to a night she relived over and over in her dreams, a restlessness in her blood she couldn't quell, to wanting things she shouldn't want.

She had a list for a reason, a template for a sensible, quiet, settled life. This year couldn't be allowed to disrupt that, no matter what her body wanted.

But it was getting harder and harder to remember that.

Willow was uncharacteristically quiet on their walk. It hadn't taken Logan long to realise just how much she adored living practically on the beach. On the few occasions he had accompanied her on her regular communes with the ocean, she had been full of thoughts and questions, but this evening she stayed mute, answering his attempts at conversation with monosyllables. Not that he tried very hard. The thought of the meal ahead dominated his thoughts, what it would be like to be face-to-face with Nate, with the consequences of his actions regarding. Although he should be used to that by now, because the other consequence was by his side. Willow was a constant reminder of the damage he wrought so thoughtlessly.

It was hard to pinpoint when the time they had spent together in Vegas had spiralled out of control. Saving her from what might have been a very nasty accident was one thing, taking her for a drink to help with her shock reasonable, and tempting her to sample some of Vegas's dubious pleasures understandable, but marriage? All Logan knew was that they seemed to have been heading towards that chapel from the moment he put the first chips in her hand, and that when she took his hand and said 'I do,' it had felt right in a way he would never be able to explain.

The twenty hours they had spent together had been the happiest in his life. No wonder he had wanted to hold on to them, even if it was just for one night, with a marriage they both knew would be dissolved before the ink really had a chance to dry.

Good God, he was pathetic! Commitment possible only if it was temporary.

Which is why much as he had wanted to cross the study earlier, to hold Willow once again, the memory of kissing her and touching her pounding through his body, he had stayed right there in his seat. She wouldn't have pushed him away. He knew that by her dilated pupils, her immobility, so he had to make sure that this time he didn't tempt her into something she'd regret.

Logan's chest tightened as they approached the all-too-familiar Inn, and he was equally relieved and surprised when Willow took his hand and squeezed his fingers reassuringly.

'What a stunning view,' was all she said, her tone light, normal, as if she didn't know his inner turmoil.

'Yes.' He was grateful for the conversational opening. 'My ancestors had an eye for the best plots. Lookout House has the best situation in the town. We've had several developers offering to buy it over the years, more with an eye on the plot and the build potential there rather than the house itself. And Great-Great-Grandfather Byrne knew what he was doing when he established The Harbour Inn.'

The Inn was an attractive white two-storey building at one end of the harbour, overlooking the natural curve of the bay. Roof terraces, balconies and a large garden meant plenty of outside space in summer, whilst inside, the ground floor was dominated by the oval bar in the middle of the room. Tables were grouped around the room edges and in every corner and nook. A stage and dance floor were permanent fixtures at one end, and upstairs were more tables. The building next door also belonged to the Byrnes, with guest quarters in cottages at the back.

Logan knew every inch of the Inn, just as he knew every inch of Lookout House. He had been partly brought up here, at first by his mother, who had preferred to spend her days with her family rather than rattle around the huge mansion, and partly because after her death, it had been a refuge away from his father's coldness.

But it wasn't his home—and he had never felt that so acutely. 'Okay then.'

With a confidence he didn't feel, he opened the door and held it, allowing Willow to precede him into the room, conscious of a swell of pride as she stepped past him. She was simply dressed in a long denim skirt teamed with a flowery top, her hair loose, but she looked elegant and self-possessed, even though he knew in reality she was a little self-conscious about meeting the rest of his family.

The season had yet to start, but Fridays were usually busy all year round, and the downstairs was already a third full. Groups of friends sat around tables, and families enjoyed the platters of food The Harbour Inn was renowned for. Logan breathed in the familiar scent of fried food, beer and salt air, and some of his trepidation faded away. It was a smell he associated with love and laughter and kindness. With family.

He just hoped that hadn't changed.

He nodded at a group of Lona workers shifting self-consciously in the corner. He'd have to send them a round. No one wanted the boss intruding on the Friday night winddown. He smiled at a few acquaintances eyeing Willow with undisguised curiosity. He had never brought a date or a girlfriend here before, not to Romney, to the Inn or Lookout House, not past high school anyway. His life was all about separation, and that's the way he'd preferred it. But now Willow was here, those barriers were crumbling.

'Logan!' His uncle greeted him from the other side of the bar. 'We were beginning to think you'd moved to England with your secret wife. Your aunt has a few words to say about that, by the way. No wonder you've been avoiding us. Time you took your punishment like a Byrne, young man.' He leaned over the polished wooden counter and held out a hand to Willow with a welcoming smile. 'Connor Byrne.'

'Willow Jones.' Willow took the proffered hand, answering the smile with one of her own as his uncle let out a low whistle.

'Jones, eh?' He winked at Logan. 'Bet your old man's spitting about that. Has he started on about grandchildren's surnames yet? He will, and don't think he'll be happy with a double barrel. He wouldn't allow your mother to give you Byrne as a middle name.'

It was an old grievance, and Logan didn't rise to it. There was no love lost between the two sides of his family. The Hartwells had thought the Byrnes below them, certainly not good enough to marry into their dynasty. The Byrnes considered the Hartwells to be incomers, no better than the summer visitors thanks to their wealth and attitude, although in reality they'd moved to the area around the same time.

'We haven't discussed it.'

'Oh, you will.'

'It's Willow's decision if and when it's an

issue,' Logan said lightly, and his uncle gave him a keen glance.

'As it should be. It's lovely to meet you, Willow. Welcome to Romney and welcome to the family. Take a seat, both of you, and I'll bring menus over—a big table, mind. Your aunt will be through, and she'll want to settle in to interrogate Willow properly.'

'And Nate?' Logan's breath caught in his throat. He didn't usually need to check in with his cousin. 'I didn't tell him we were coming…it was all a bit last-minute. Is he around to join us?''

His uncle rubbed his chin thoughtfully. 'He's at home. Truth is, it would do him good to get out. He's a bit self-conscious on those sticks at the moment, but he'll want to meet Willow. Why don't you go and ask him? I'll keep your bride company.'

Before Logan had a chance to check with Willow, his uncle had called to one of the waitresses to take his place at the bar and was shepherding Willow towards a secluded corner table, screened off from the rest of the room. Grateful to his uncle for ensuring that Willow wouldn't spend the evening being stared at by the curious patrons, Logan made his way through the door separating the kitchen from the bar and then into the yard which connected the two buildings. As usual. the back door was unlocked and Logan walked straight into the combined kitchen dining and family room which was the heart of the Byrne house. It was light and airy, a little cluttered with photos, trophies and pictures. Nate was the light of his parents' life and it showed, his art showcased from first scribbles and messy collages to the simple but moving line drawings he did to relax. There were photos of Logan too, of course. After all, he had eaten half his childhood meals in this house, slept in the small room under the eaves countless times. Up until now he had never doubted his welcome.

As always, he stopped by a framed picture in pride of place just inside the door. Blond tangled hair stiff with salt, eyes crinkling against the sun, smile wide and unfettered. His mother at just twenty-two, the summer before the local lord of the manor had decided he must have her—only to try and clip her wings the instant he possessed her. If his father had been a different man, would she be alive now? Logan knew she had stormed out of the house after one of their many arguments, taken her horse out in a rage. Had all that emotion made her reckless? His father was right. Logan had inherited her nature.

Had allowed impulsivity and emotion to rule his actions, and once again the consequences were life-changing.

'Aunt Sofia,' he called.

'Logan? I thought I heard someone come in.' Sofia Byrne bustled in and, to Logan's relief, enveloped him in a huge hug before stepping back and peering up at him severely. 'What's this about you getting married? When? Where? Who? And where is she?' His aunt peered around as if he might have Willow concealed behind him.

'In the bar with Uncle Connor. He's keeping her company until you get there.'

'She's here? Why didn't you say so? Nate is in the den. Bring him with you.' She stepped back and looked up at him searchingly. 'You look well, Logan. This girl suits you.' And with a squeeze of his arm, she was gone, leaving Nate alone in the kitchen, ready to face his business partner, best friend and cousin.

The den was a cosy room at the back of the house usually used for watching television on winter nights when the sea stormed and rain pelted down. As Logan approached, he saw it had been made over into a temporary bedroom. Nate was sprawled on the sofa, his leg stretched out in front of him, crutches lying within easy reach. Logan took a moment to survey his cousin. His dark hair was a little longer than usual, there were new lines around his eyes and mouth, and his usually tanned skin, a bequest from his Portuguese maternal ancestors and his outdoors existence, greyer than usual.

'Hey man, how's it going?'

It wasn't what he wanted to say. He wanted to say, *I'm sorry, please forgive me, I nearly killed you and I will never forgive myself.* But somehow the words weren't in his vocabulary.

To his relief, Nate looked up with a genuine smile. 'You're a brave man. My mom has been cursing your name.'

Logan felt a small crack in his heart. He'd expected it, but Sofia's welcome had given him hope. 'Nate...'

'You got married without telling her? Without telling me? Logan, what the hell's going on?'

CHAPTER EIGHT

LOGAN COULD ONLY blink and stare at his cousin, unable to believe what he'd just heard. 'That's what she's mad about?'

It was Nate's turn to look surprised. 'What else? None of us have even heard of this girl, and now you're *married* to her? My mom loves you...you know that. Tried her best after your mom... Well, there's no point going over all that. She's just upset you took such a step without letting her know.'

Logan sat down heavily on the chair opposite Nate. 'It didn't occur to me.' He shook his head, trying to dislodge the thoughts all tangled together. 'I didn't think anyone would care.'

'To be honest, she's not the only one feeling out of the loop. We've been working together and surfing together and hanging out together for the last year, and you never once mentioned that you were in a long-distance relationship, let alone that you were serious enough to get married. I'm sure you had your reasons, Logan, but you can see why it's come as a shock.'

The all-too-familiar guilt pressed heavily on him. He hadn't taken his family's thoughts into consideration when coming up with his madcap scheme. His attention had been on ensuring Willow wasn't penalised, and on keeping his fractured relationship with his father from getting worse. He was so used to thinking of himself as alone that he had forgotten that there were those who cared for him.

Or maybe he just didn't dare take it for granted. Not for the first time, the lie pressed heavily on his conscience. 'I'm sorry. It was all so spur-of-the-moment. We didn't know what we thought about it, let alone anyone else.'

'I knew you weren't yourself in Hawaii, but I didn't suspect marriage. Man, no wonder you were distracted.'

And then the words flowed as they should have done from the start. 'Nate, I am so sorry. I had no right being on a board in that frame of mind. When I think what could have happened, what has happened…' He gestured to his cousin's leg. 'I thought that was why Aunt Sofia was mad—and she has every right to be.'

Nate shifted. 'So that's why you've been so odd lately? Because of my leg? I thought it was married life. Accidents happen, and to be honest, my mind wasn't where it needed to be either.'

'But if I'd been properly focused...'

'Have you been self-flagellating about this for the last few weeks?' Nate picked up a cushion and threw it directly at Logan. 'No wonder you haven't been around. Why didn't you just say something?'

'When I woke up in hospital, I was told you were in an induced coma. That you might have a serious head injury, that you might lose the use of your legs.' Logan squeezed his eyes closed, reliving that moment. 'To know it was all my fault...'

'But it wasn't,' Nate interrupted. 'I just told you. There was something I wanted to talk to you about, and I just kept putting it off. I was completely off my game. When that wave hit, I had no idea where you were. It's my fault as much as yours, maybe more.' His cousin's grin was sardonic. 'Some surf champions we are. If this got out, our brand value would plummet.'

'We'll add it to the list.' Logan meant the many years of secrets the cousins had faithfully kept, from who broke an ornament to who scraped Connor's boat. *Punish both or neither* had been their mantra. 'Are you sure you don't blame me?'

'No more than I blame myself. These things happen, Logan. We both know that every time we take a board out, or a boat, or head out for a climb. That's what makes the adrenaline rush worth it. My luck gave out this time, that's all.'

Logan sat back, feeling some of the pressure lift as he absorbed Nate's words. 'What was so important you didn't know how to talk to me about it?'

'Not marriage. That one's yours.' Nate picked up another cushion and fiddled with it for several long seconds. 'The thing is, Dad's not getting any younger. He doesn't want to retire, but he doesn't want to be behind a bar seven days a week for the rest of his life either. There's been a Byrne running The Harbour Inn for two centuries...'

'He wants you to take over?'

'You're not the only heir to a Romney empire, you know.'

'I know. But why now? Uncle Connor isn't sixty yet. What's the hurry?'

'Timing. The Surf Shack is up for sale, not officially, but Dad's been approached, and there's a cafe further up the coast to be sold at the end of the season.'

'He's thinking about expanding? Makes sense.' It did. The Harbour Inn had a good reputation, featuring in several guidebooks and even appearing in more than one travel show. Now Logan thought about it, he was only surprised they hadn't considered expanding before. The limited merchandise they sold always did well, and tables were hard to get at the height of the season.

'We've been asked if we'd consider franchising before, and do you remember that one investor who wanted to create frozen meals inspired by our menu and with our logo? Dad always refused, wanted to make sure anything with our name on had the right quality, but now he's thinking about what my future looks like, especially with Lona in the mix. Wants us to work together, for this to be a real family business.'

'And what do you want?' The million-dollar question.

'I guess this place in my blood, like HartCo is in yours. Lona has been insane, this huge wave that carried us from that shack on the beach to the kind of reach I could never have envisioned. And I never imagined earning the kind of salary we command either. That will be hard to walk away from, I have to be honest. But being the bean counter in the office doesn't suit me. I'm a doer as well as a planner. You know that. But I know you have other pulls on your time. I don't want to let you down. More importantly, I don't want to let the guys down. I'm proud of what we've built, what we contribute to the town, the opportunities we create for local people.'

'And now you want to do it all again with the Inn?' In his heart, Logan had known this day would come. Nate had never given less than one hundred per cent to Lona, but he had never needed it the way Logan had. Had never had that drive to prove himself, so much more secure in his capabilities.

'I think I do.'

'If you needed capital to expand the Inn, we could sell Lona.' It hurt to say the words, but he had to offer.

'And risk letting the manufacturing and the offices leave Romney?' Nate shook his head. 'I couldn't do that.'

'It's not my preferred option either. It would make most sense for us to both stay on the board and appoint a CEO and an operations director to do the day-to-day.' It would be difficult to hand the company they'd built up over to new blood, but at least this way they'd still be involved. 'How long have you been thinking about this? Why haven't you mentioned this before, Nate?'

Nate shifted, looking uncomfortable. 'I know how important Lona is to you. I didn't want to let you down. But now you're spending more time at HartCo, now you're married, now Dad's got this opportunity, the time seems right...'

'Everything's changing,' Logan agreed with a pang of nostalgia for the two teens who had followed their passion, the young men who had grown a small, specialised business into a global brand. 'Guess it was bound to happen sooner or later. Come on, I've left Willow alone with your parents for too long, and I have instructions to get you to leave this room. It's time for you to meet my wife.'

'I like your family. I had a lovely evening. Thanks for agreeing to it.' Willow pressed a hand against her stomach and winced. 'I just wish I had had the strength to say no to dessert.'

'And hurt my uncle's feelings?' Logan grinned at her. 'You're too polite for that.' He started to walk along the road away from the Inn and she fell into step beside him.

'I'm still adjusting to American portions.

I need to go retro and just order a starter if I want pudding. But then I would have missed out on the fish platter...'

'Unthinkable. It's the house speciality.' She sensed him slant a glance at her. 'They really liked you too. All three pulled me aside at some point to tell me they approve.'

'Really? They didn't think I was too English? Too reserved?'

'Classy, my aunt said.'

'I'll take that.'

'You did really well. I know it must have been overwhelming, especially under the circumstances.'

'It was a bit embarrassing when your aunt kept asking for details about how we met. I don't mind fudging details, but I don't want to lie outright more than is absolutely necessary.' It was bad enough with Logan's father, who, although he was much more polite to her than to his son, had made no effort to find out more about how his new daughter-in-law had entered the family, but she found it much harder selling their story to people who clearly cared about Logan very much and only wanted his happiness and were full of questions as a result.

'I know. I wish...' He stopped.

'Wish what?'

'I wish we could be honest with them. After all, I know they wouldn't say anything to my father. I had good reasons for asking you to come and spend this year with me...'

'Bribed me, you mean.' She touched his arm to show she was joking, and he took her hand in his. The feel of skin on skin consumed her, all her focus shooting to their linked fingers. Willow took a deep breath and tried to concentrate on the conversation.

'Paid you,' Logan countered with a half smile. 'I needed to protect you after blurting out that we were married, and I didn't want to sever what little relationship my father and I do have. Of course, the irony is that marrying you is the only thing I have ever done he approves of.'

She could hear him trying for levity, and it almost physically hurt. Logan might pretend that he didn't care about his father's disapproval, but she could see through his mask, was aware just how much it did hurt him. 'I'm sure that's not true.' But the awful truth was, she wasn't sure at all.

'It is, and that's fine. But what I'm saying is, those reasons still stand, but I know there's more to it than that. I know that you are embarrassed about Vegas, that you don't want people to know what really happened, and I get that. Which is why although I wish we could be honest with them, I am happy to lie to protect you, even to my aunt and uncle. Even to Nate. Awkward as their happiness and questions are.'

Willow couldn't answer, didn't know what to say, but she was touched by his words, by the sentiment behind them. Even more, she was shocked by his perception, by how much he seemed to know her, to see her. 'This is why I haven't told my sister or my parents anything about us,' she said at last. 'It's not just the lying. It's knowing they'd be so excited for me, so happy, and that I wouldn't deserve that happiness. I felt the same way during that meal. But honestly, I think telling your family the truth now would be worse. It would take away that joy to salve our consciences. We just need to suck up feeling bad and deal with it.'

'What's your plan where your family is concerned?'

'I don't know,' she admitted. 'To be honest, I try not to think about it, and when I do, I tell myself that there's no reason for them to ever know, that it's not like they will come and visit this year or are likely to meet anyone who knows us. But at the same time, I know I'm just kidding myself. I can't pretend

this year never happened. I just need to figure out what to tell them and when. It's not
like me to put difficult things off, but this
one is tricky.' Too tricky for her to figure out
alone. And yet she was used to being alone.
Preferred it. Didn't she?

'You can talk to me. Any time.' It was as
if he had read her mind.

'I know,' she half whispered. 'I do know
that, Logan.'

They carried on walking along the coastal
road that curved its way into town in silence,
hands still linked, Willow's mind racing with
the events of the evening, the moment in the
study, the friendly meal, the realisation that
the more time she spent with Logan, the more
she understood him, the more she opened up
to him, the harder it was to keep her distance.

'It's a nice evening,' she said at last. 'Want
to walk the rest of the way along the beach?'

'Sure.'

There were no street lights lighting the way
once they left the road, but the moon was out,
and several boats were brightly illuminated
anchored out at sea, creating enough light
to see by as they made their way along the
beach. She sought for something to say that
didn't bring the conversation back to their

situation. 'So you and Nate are going to hand over control of Lona.'

'It seems that it's time.'

'How do you feel about that?'

'Conflicted,' he admitted. 'I always knew I would need to step back at some point, but I thought Nate would still be there at the helm. But I'm glad he doesn't want to sell. I might have bought him out rather than let it go into other hands, but it wouldn't have been the same without him. Actually, I was thinking that if we're moving to a more formal structure, that you might want to sit on the board of directors. Your financial eye might be very useful.'

'I don't know anything about surfboards!' But she was touched by the suggestion.

'You don't need to, although I am happy to give you some lessons. You do understand risk and financial security and accounts, and you're not as close to the business as Nate and I. You're more likely to be able to take a neutral viewpoint, which will be useful as we learn to take a step back.'

'In that case, I'd love to. Thank you.' She didn't ask what would happen when her year was up, whether she would still be wanted when she was no longer his wife. It all felt so far away.

The evening was cool, and Willow was glad of her coat as they continued along the shore, stopping by unspoken accord to look out at the moonlit ocean. 'It's so beautiful here,' she said.

'I'm glad you like it.'

'More than like, I love it. In spite of everything, I feel at home on the coast, which is odd, because I have never lived by the sea before.'

'But you did live on water,' he pointed out. 'And your dream house overlooks a canal.'

'Canals seem so tame compared with the ocean.' She felt melancholy, the cottage of her dreams fading away to be replaced by a house on a beach. She was changing, even in the short time she'd spent here, evolving into someone new. She'd worked so hard to control every aspect of her life, and she could feel that control slipping, new wants and desires and dreams replacing all she had striven for. It was exhilarating and terrifying in equal measure. Part of her wanted to turn the clock back to before Vegas, to when she had been on track, to when life was safe. But given the choice, she knew she wouldn't, because for all her fear and regret, she couldn't deny that for the first time in a long time, she felt fully alive—and she knew a great deal of that was down to the man standing next to her, still holding her hand.

'Can I ask you something?' Logan broke the silence. It was so dim she couldn't make out his expression.

'Of course.'

'Why did you say yes?'

'To what?'

'To marrying me.'

Willow froze. It was of course the million-dollar question, the reason they were here, the reason her life was spiralling far from where it should be.

'Why did you ask me?' she countered.

'It felt right.'

She put that information to one side to consider more deeply at another time. 'To me too.' But she knew that wasn't enough of an answer. 'I've asked myself that question a lot. Marrying a man you'd known for less than one day would be reckless for anyone, but for me it was like I was someone else entirely. And I was that day.' She stopped and thought about what she'd just said. 'No, that's too easy a get-out. I was the me I don't allow myself to be.'

'Okay,' he said slowly, and she could feel him try to understand.

She took a deep breath, carefully disentangling her thoughts and memories and feelings. 'Control is important to me, Logan. Direction, perseverance, hard work, they are all important too, but control is everything. I need to know that my life is in my hands, hence the goals and the checklist. But there are times when I can't help but wonder what life would be like if I was like my sister, my parents, if I could just live without worrying about the consequences and tear up the to-do list.'

His hand tightened on hers, the only indication that he was listening. She was glad of the dark, that she was looking out at the distant boats, that she couldn't see his expression.

'Skye and I had had an argument. It was silly, forgotten by the time I returned. But during it, she said that she felt sorry for me, sorry for the narrowness of my life, for all the roads untaken because I only ever looked straight ahead. I was *so* mad with her, and although I didn't acknowledge it, I was mostly mad because she hit a nerve. What *would* my life have been like if I hadn't always been the sensible one? If I allowed myself to live for the moment like the rest of my family?'

'For what it's worth,' Logan said in a low voice, 'I think you're pretty much perfect the way you are.'

She laughed at that. 'I'm not even close, but thank you for saying that. Then in Vegas, everyone else was partying while I was up in my room, passive aggressively sending emails all evening to prove that I at least was behaving responsibly and to try and drown out Skye's words. If I stopped, they were all I could hear. And then you pulled me back from that car, and I realised that if it had hit me, what would have been my legacy? An email sent at midnight? A CV full of qualifications but no actual living?'

'A loving daughter, sister and aunt who put her family first. That's not such a bad legacy.'

'You challenged me.' She didn't even know what she was saying now. 'It was as if you saw through the facade to the person I didn't know how to be, was too scared to admit even existed. It felt safe to let go with you.' She stopped, trying to articulate the way she had felt that day, as if he were a safety net allowing her to soar from her self-imposed cage. 'I felt seen in a way I had never felt seen before. The men I dated only saw the Willow I wanted them to see. They liked the to-do lists and the life plans and the work ethic, because they were the same. I knew that if I ever did marry, then I would marry one of them, and impulsive Willow would be buried forever. I just wanted her to have one day. To let her loose and to do all the things I would never do, no matter how foolish. She would have married you like a shot—and meant it whether for one night, one week or as long as it was right, without thinking of the many reasons it was a bad idea. And so I said yes. I said yes to it all, even that zip line.'

'It was the wedding crashing I thought you were going to balk at.'

'Crashing that dental conference was one thing, but weddings did feel a step too far— but I saw you pay the bar bill when we left.'

'Stealing a dance is one thing, but someone else's food and drink is another. Willow?' He sounded serious, and she turned to him.

'Mmm?'

'Impulsive Willow said yes, but did you?'

She stared at him for a moment, wanting, needing to be honest, touched by his need for truth. 'Do you remember what you said to me in the casino? When you gave me those chips?'

'Don't bet it all on red?'

She laughed. 'You told me that the key to gambling, whether it's money or business, is to know what you are willing to lose and stop there. They're wise words, Logan. I said yes that day, but I knew what I was—and wasn't—

willing to lose. And I don't regret it.' Willow didn't know until she said the words that she meant them. 'I don't regret a minute of that day, and I don't regret that I am here with you now. I know it's not real, and I know we don't have a future, and I hate the lying, but I don't regret it. Because I still feel seen. And that's rare for me. Precious.'

She had no idea who moved first, but before she had finished speaking, she was in his arms, and his mouth was claiming hers as if she was really his—and in that moment, she was. She pushed herself close to him, burying her hands in his hair to pull him even tighter against her, her body aching with impatience and anticipation.

That night in Vegas, his kisses had been at first sweet and then incendiary. These kisses were hungry, demanding, and she gave back in full measure, lost in the feel, the taste of him, the roar of the surf mingling with the pounding of her pulse. Impatient, she pulled at his coat, only for Logan to pull away, capturing her hands in his.

'Sex on the beach isn't all it's cracked up to be, especially in this weather.'

Willow was shocked by the wave of jealousy which broke over her at the realisation he was speaking from experience. He was a rich, attractive thirty-year-old man. There were probably few places where he hadn't had sex. The haze of desire cleared a little.

'But…' He traced a hand down her cheek and across her lips, and her sensitised skin flamed where he touched. 'That doesn't mean we don't have options. There's our apartment, of course, or my boat…'

'You have a boat here?'

'In the harbour.'

'Show me.' She knew they would make love, that there was no other way for this evening to end, but she wasn't quite ready to share a marital bed with him, to take that step. A boat was a halfway house, a place to unleash these feelings which had overwhelmed her without making any promises for the future.

'You're sure?' He cupped her face in his hands, looking searchingly into her eyes.

'Are you?' Some of the certainty dissolved. Maybe he didn't want her after all, but his wolfish smile dispelled the doubts.

'More than anything.'

'Then let's go.'

CHAPTER NINE

IN NORMAL TIMES, Willow would have wanted to explore the elegant little boat. Brought up on one, she was always intrigued by different layouts, and this ocean-going cruiser was cleverly and luxuriously laid out in a way that was very different to her rather hippy-ish childhood home. But she couldn't allow herself to stop, because if she did, she would stop altogether. All the reasons why this was such a bad idea would come flooding back and drown out the part of her who insisted this was the inevitable destination.

And why not? They were married, after all. They had ensured there could be no annulment for nonconsummation on their wedding night, so what was the point of sleeping alone in frustrated chastity? There had to be some benefits to this marriage. She liked Logan. She was attracted to him. He made her feel both beautiful and seen. Just because there was an end date on their union didn't mean they couldn't enjoy it while it lasted.

The cabin was surprisingly large, dominated by the double bed, made up with white linen. 'It's all so tidy,' she said, a little surprised by the polished wood and clean linen. Logan hadn't had a chance to take the boat out since they'd returned from London as far as she knew.

Logan didn't answer. He'd not said much since she had suggested they come here, and now they were standing in the lamplit cabin, she couldn't read him at all. It hadn't been like this in Vegas. There he had swept her back to his hotel room, where he had ordered champagne that neither of them touched, too caught up in each other to need any outside stimulus. There had been no hesitancy, no awkwardness. It had felt so natural, so right. Now Willow was thinking that she could very much do with a drink. They stood and stared at each other, two wary animals, each waiting for the other to move.

'This is awkward,' Willow said at last, needing to break the ice. 'Shall we go back to the beach?'

To her relief, her words did the trick, and Logan smiled at last, a little rueful, a little appreciative. 'I just don't want you to have any regrets.'

'I thought we sorted that out on the beach,' she said. 'And it's a little too late for regrets anyway.'

'I don't want to hurt you…'

'Oh, I see. You think one more night with you and I will fall desperately in love and have my heart broken. You're very sure of yourself, Logan Prestwood Hartwell.' She put a hand on her hip, shaking her hair back. 'Maybe you'll be the one who falls in love with *me*. Maybe that's what you should be worried about.'

She was joking of course, but she could see want and regret and desolation glimmer in his eyes for one second, so brief she thought she had imagined it. 'I don't think love is for me,' he said so quietly she could barely make out the words. 'But if it was, I would be in real danger.'

All Willow wanted to do was wipe away the pain in his voice, and so she boldly moved towards him, all doubt and awkwardness gone as she took his face in her hands, looking up at him, at the dark blue eyes, the straight, almost stern eyebrows, the hollows in his cheeks, the line of his jaw, the curve of his mouth, before standing on her tiptoes to press her mouth to his, taking charge in a way she had never done before. Logan was immobile as she pressed teasing kisses to his mouth, whispering them along his jaw and to his neck then back again, enjoying the scent of him, the taste of him, the thrill of being in control. She stood back and unzipped her coat, tossed it onto the chair, and then stood back. 'Now you.'

Logan looked at her expressionlessly for one long moment, then complied. Willow nodded. 'Now your sweater,' she told him, and a glint of appreciation lit up his face as he pulled it off in one graceful movement, his T-shirt riding up as he did so. A jolt of desire shot through her, pooling deep down in her belly at the exposed hint of toned, tanned stomach.

Still looking directly at him she unbuttoned her top and shrugged it off, then did the same to her skirt, quickly unrolling her tights and stepping out of them, toeing them to one side. She refused to feel exposed or embarrassed clad in just her bra and pants, instead she raised an eyebrow.

'What are you waiting for?'

'I'm just taking a moment to admire the view.'

Her natural instinct was to hide, to use her hands to futilely cover herself, to slip under sheets, but instead she stood still, allowing his gaze to roam over her, luxuriating in her power as his eyes darkened even more, almost black with desire and he visibly swallowed.

She willed her voice not to waver. 'You've had long enough. My turn.'

His mouth quirked in amusement, but he didn't delay any longer, stripping off his T-shirt. Willow sucked in a breath as she took in clearly defined pecs, strong stomach muscles, toned biceps. There was a lot to be said for marrying an adrenaline junkie addicted to outdoor exercise. But she made herself stay still, did her best to sound cool despite the excitement thrumming through her veins. 'And the rest.'

Slowly, holding her gaze the whole time, Logan undid his belt buckle before unbuttoning his fly, letting his jeans fall down by his ankles. He stepped out of them unhurriedly. 'What now?'

He was letting her call the shots. For one frantic moment, Willow wished she had never started this, that she had let him lead, as she had with her boyfriends in the past, unconfident in her sexuality, unsure of her needs, embarrassed to articulate her desires. But at the same time, his trust in her, evident want of her, understanding of her were a heady brew, and Willow knew that she would regret not taking advantage of it.

She walked towards him, slow and measured, stopping a few inches away. Keeping her eyes fixed on his, she allowed herself to explore the lines of his face, the hard muscle and cords of his neck and arms, the planes of his back and chest. Lower and yet lower she allowed her fingers to trail in this delicious, tantalising discovery, not an inch left untouched. She circled round, spiralling slowly round him as her fingers danced over his torso. His eyes were half-closed, his breathing visible and audible, and at times he quivered as she stroked and caressed, but he didn't move.

Finally she was back where she had started, looking up at him. She placed her hands on his chest and manoeuvred him back step by step until they reached the bed. She gently pushed him down so he sat on the edge of the bed, and then she moved to stand between his legs, looking down at him. She could barely breathe, barely think. Her whole body was on fire, need and want and desire colliding in a delicious pain burning through her. Looking deep into Logan's eyes, seeing the almost heroic self-control he was exerting, almost undid her. Once again she cupped his face in her hands and kissed him. The effect was incendiary. In seconds control was forgotten, all games discarded as she melted into him, falling onto him. She explored with abandon now, all embarrassment and constraint gone, arching into him as he did the same, white-hot flames flaring at the contact.

Now he was touching her too, not with the delicate, teasing caresses she had employed but with an all-consuming greed, his hands, his mouth everywhere as he stripped off her underwear, discarding his in a move so swift she barely noticed. She was still on top but no longer in control, lost in a haze of lust as he touched and licked and kissed. He murmured endearments as he relearnt her, hissing in sharp breaths as she relearnt him in turn. She luxuriated in the feel of him underneath her, running her tongue along his shoulder and down his chest, her hands gripping his shoulders as he did the same, nibbling and kissing his way down her body, bringing her closer and closer to the edge, before returning to her neck, her breasts as his clever, clever hands made her body soar. Her breath was coming in shallow pants, sweat slick on her skin, her mind spiralling up to the stars and beyond. She came back to, finding herself on her back, wrapping her arms, her legs around him and urging him closer, closer still.

Logan stilled and raised himself onto his forearms, looking deep into her eyes. 'Is this okay?' he half growled, the tension clear on his face. She knew that even as far as they had come, one word from her and he would immediately desist without a murmur. That she still had all the control.

'More than okay.' And it was. Whatever was to come in this strange marriage of theirs, she couldn't, wouldn't regret this night.

And best of all, it had only just started.

'Hey, I got you coffee.'

Logan woke with a start, unsure for a moment where he was, gazing at the panelled walls and porthole in confusion before his mind cleared and he remembered everything. His conversation with Nate, the reassurance that his aunt and uncle weren't furious with him, the moment he had asked Willow the question that had been consuming him for the last two months.

Why me?

Logan knew what most people thought about him. Lucky, rich, sporty, devil-may-care. Husband material because of his lineage and inheritance, not because of who he was. Not that he'd ever got close to marriage before. His relationships never lasted long enough. He was too much of a closed book, they said, too selfish. Too unpindownable with his schedule of competitions taking him away from the annual events where men like him were supposed to see and be seen. Despite this, he'd always thought he would end up making his old man's dreams come true and end up with some East Coast heiress who had no interest in his inner life as long as she had receptions to host and the right charity boards to sit on. The thought gave him no pleasure, but he knew what the consequences of imprisoning the wrong kind of woman inside his gilded cage were.

His mother's memory was a constant reminder.

Which was why he needed to ensure Willow got her freedom at the end of this year. She set herself too many limits to be confined by more. But when she did let go, she was sensational…

A slow smile crept over his face as he turned to look at his wife. 'You look far too dressed,' he said. She was back in the skirt and buttoned-up blouse, her hair neatly combed and her face washed.

'I could hardly have got coffee undressed,'

she told him with a blush, setting the paper bag she carried onto the bedside table. 'And I got pastries.'

'You are an exemplary wife.' He grabbed her hand and pulled her, half protesting and half laughing, onto the bed. 'How did I get so lucky?'

The coffee was almost cold by the time they finally got round to drinking it, but it was a small price to pay. 'I'll buy you a new one,' he called out to the galley, setting the cup down, picking up one of the paper bags and peeking inside. 'Pastéis de nata, my favourite.'

'So indulgent, I know, but they are as good as the ones I had in Lisbon.' Willow appeared with two plates and held one out to him. He didn't attempt to suppress a smile. So prim and proper in so many ways, whereas in others…look at her now, hair tangled around her face, lips swollen, wearing one of his sailing polo shirts, big on her, only just covering her perfect bottom, yet she was still careful not to get crumbs on the rumpled sheets.

'Lisbon. One of your ten European capitals?'

'I can't believe you remembered that.'

'I forget nothing,' he promised her. 'Where else have you been?'

Willow sat on the end of the bed and took

the bag he handed her, tipping her own pastry onto her plate.

'Paris was the first. At nineteen. First I saved for a passport, then my Eurostar ticket. I went in October because it was cheaper, so it was autumnal, a bit drizzly, utterly beautiful. Just like I'd imagined. I had little money so I mostly wandered around, stopping for cafe au lait and *le menu prix fixe*.' Her voice was soft with nostalgia. 'I went back again, when I earned more, so I could actually go inside some of the museums, eat in the renowned restaurants, go to Versailles, and it was wonderful, but there was something very special about that first trip.'

'I can imagine.' But he couldn't, not really. One thing Logan had never lacked was money. He could—and did—travel anywhere he liked, and while there stay in the best places, eat at the fanciest restaurants, indulge in any activity he chose. And no one memory was as special to him as Paris clearly was to her.

'Brussels next and then Amsterdam, thanks to those Eurostar deals, also out of season and on the cheap. My employer gave me a bonus when I finished my degree, and for once it didn't go straight into my house fund. Instead I treated myself to a trip to Rome.' Her eyes shone with the memory. 'I was so worried it wouldn't meet my expectations, but it exceeded them. Standing in the Forum, surrounded by ghosts two millennia old...'

'Rome's incredible.' Again he felt that pang of envy. That ability to wring so much pleasure from just being somewhere was nothing he had ever experienced. Willow didn't need competition or adrenaline to enjoy a place. She didn't need the fanciest hotels or most expensive restaurants. She just needed to be part of it. 'So, city breaks only? You never let loose on a beach? No partying in Ibiza or yachting around Greek islands?'

'The thing is,' she confessed, 'I felt guilty taking holidays. There's always so much to do. But if it's educational...'

'At some point this year, you and I are going to go on a vacation that is nothing but pure relaxation,' he said, and was rewarded by a rosy flush on her cheeks and an almost shy smile.

'I'd like that. At least,' she added cautiously, 'for a bit. I'm not sure I am made for doing nothing for too long.'

'I'll make sure you pack an improving book. Talking of leisure, what shall we do with the rest of the weekend? I owe you a hot coffee for a start. What?' Willow was looking at him in evident surprise. 'Do I have custard on my face?'

'No, but you don't normally take the weekend off.' She frowned. 'It makes no sense, does it?'

'What doesn't?'

'Why your father talks to you the way he does, as if you do nothing but drink and party and seduce women.'

'Happy to be currently guilty of the third of those.'

Willow didn't dignify him with a response. 'You clearly have put a huge amount of time into Lona...'

'Ah, but a lot of that time was demonstrating what our boards and kit do. If it's fun, it's not work, according to my respected father.'

'And over the last few weeks, you stepped into a new role at HartCo whilst covering for Nate and your own old job. Hence the working weekends and late nights. No one would have blamed you for sorting out the succession at Lona before taking on the HartCo responsibilities.'

'Maybe you're not the only one who likes to be busy.' She was right, of course. He could quite easily have taken six months to succession plan, recruit and train someone to replace him, before starting the expanded role in the family business, but once the decision had been made, he'd wanted to get stuck in at HartCo, not give himself time to regret it. And much as he disliked to admit it, part of him had hoped maybe his father would notice that he was putting in all the hours, all the effort. It was a vain hope, but where his father was concerned, weren't they all?

'Why though? Were you a particularly wild child? Did you lose over half of HartCo in a bet? Embezzle it away? Give away trade secrets? I just can't marry up what I see with what I hear. The hostility between you…' She stopped. 'I'm sorry, it's none of my business.'

'You live with us. It's completely your business,' Logan said. 'And actually, Dad and I have been pretty civil to each other recently. You're a good influence on him.'

'This is civil?' He couldn't bear the pity in her eyes and took a long gulp of cold coffee. 'No wonder you travelled around so much. Didn't you ever think of moving out?'

'All the time.' He put the cup down and lay back down, arms behind his head, to stare at the low wooden ceiling. 'I've always had boltholes, of course. My room at Connor and Sofia's, here, school and college, travelling for work as much as I did. I've probably spent less than a quarter of my time at Lookout

House since my mother died. In fact, I don't think I have spent as many nights there as I have over the last couple of months.' He looked over at Willow sitting straight-backed at the end of the bed, irresistibly rumpled. 'Are you comfortable there?' He patted the bed with a suggestive grin, but she wasn't biting—this time.

'Quite comfortable, thanks. So it just didn't seem worth getting a place of your own?'

She was clearly not going to give up this line of enquiry easily. 'When I was young, I always thought I'd move to a city—New York maybe, not Boston, or somewhere abroad, and break those Hartwell traditions—but of course it was clear when I graduated that Lona had the potential to be something special. The workshop was here, Nate was here, our branding was all about here. And Hartwells live at Lookout House. It's my home. Why should I be driven out?'

What he couldn't—and was sure he wanted to—explain was how fiercely, despite everything, he wanted to belong. To not be an outsider despite his every effort to be. And he loved his large, quirky, beachside home with its turrets and gables and folksy-cottage-meets-castle charm. 'It's not as if there isn't room for eight families to live there. That was what it was designed for. I can go a whole week without even hearing Dad.'

'True. I suppose it's not as if you're crammed into a tiny apartment with him.'

'And until a few years ago, my grandparents were there too. My dad wasn't any easier to please, but he and his dad had their own issues. Took the heat off me a bit.'

'Three warring generations instead of two. What a fun prospect. Did you get on with your grandparents?'

'I loved them…' He paused. If only it were that simple.

'I sense a but…?'

'No buts. I loved them and they loved me. They were proud of me and they showed it. But…' He smiled wryly. 'Okay, maybe *one* but. They were very old school, more than a bit *them* and *us*. There's a lot of historic snobbery in Romney. Not much mixing between the year-rounders and the summer visitors, and as far as my grandparents were concerned, Hartwells were not townsfolk.'

'But you live there all year round.'

'Which just goes to show how ridiculous it is. But the enmity is on both sides. The townsfolk like the tourist dollars but not the attitude and the inflated prices, and the summer visitors aren't so much hostile as entitled and sometimes downright rude. Anyway, my grandparents disapproved of my parents' marriage. Partly because she was the daughter of the local bar owner and worked there, partly because she hadn't been to college, partly because she had no intention of being moulded into a Hartwell wife. I don't think they made life easy for my mother—and to be fair, I don't think she made life easy for them. She hated all the society expectations, the fundraisers and events, the etiquette. She liked to spend her evenings behind the bar of The Harbour Inn and her days out at sea or surfing or riding even when she was married. Especially when she was married. There doesn't seem to have been any compromise on either side.' He looked up at the ceiling again, trying to push back the pain and loneliness and loss that engulfed him whenever he thought about his mother. 'I wish she was still here, so I could ask her about that time. After she died, no one really talked about her, no Hartwells I mean.'

'I'm sorry, Logan.'

'It was a long time ago. I mean, I barely remember her.' He tried for a light tone but could see by the empathy on her face he'd failed.

'You must miss her.'

'Yes,' he admitted. 'I do. But I wasn't unhappy, Willow. Don't think of me as a lonely little boy rattling around that house. I had my grandparents, I had my uncle and aunt and Nate, I had friends here in the town. As I got older, I had my boat and board. I've had opportunities most kids can't even dream of.' But that wasn't exactly true. There were times when Lookout House had felt very lonely indeed, times when yearning for his mother had been physically painful.

'I know.' Her expression was still troubled as she stood up and put her plate down on the small table by the door before getting back onto the bed and folding herself in next to him, her body warm against his. 'But having all of those opportunities doesn't mean you're not allowed to grieve what you lost. Do you think it would be different with your father if your mother had lived?'

'Now, that is the million-dollar question.' Logan slipped an arm around her, pulling Willow in close. He'd never talked to anyone outside his mother's family about his childhood before, slipping away from questions with an ease born of long practice, but she deserved as much honesty as he could manage. 'I can't imagine the marriage surviving, and I can't imagine any custody battle being resolved amicably, but who knows? My father loved her once—or more likely, he was infatuated with her. She was very beautiful, wild, charismatic. You can see the appeal to a preppy young man who had been brought up in society, that whole wrong-side-of-the-tracks thing. Until they were actually married, and then he just wanted her to fit in. That's why he's always been hard on me. He sees any trace of her in me as a failure, a reminder of his mistakes.'

'And that's on him, Logan.' She cupped his cheek, forcing him to turn and look at her. 'Not on you. The Logan he sees isn't the Logan anyone else sees. He views you through a lens of his own self-loathing, his regrets. You can't let it define you.'

'I know.' But the truth was, he had let it define him. Nothing he achieved had ever felt good enough, not just to his father, but to Logan himself. 'It's just try as I might, part of me is waiting for him to be proud of me. To tell me I'm good enough. I know it's pathetic.'

'No, it's not pathetic.' Her hands were warm, soft, comfort incarnate. 'We all yearn for what we didn't have. I would give anything to be able to lay my problems down at my parents' feet sometimes. To say *I messed up, help me*. To tell Skye about Vegas and get her advice. To not have to be the strong one, the sensible one, just occasionally. Just wanting that makes me feel weak, but it's okay to want, Logan. It is.'

'And right now, I want you.' He did, in a way that was all-consuming, different to last night's desire-driven passion or the morning's sweet, fun-filled love-making. Darker, needier, this came from the depths of a soul he denied was lonely.

'You have me,' she half whispered as he took her mouth with his, kissing her hard as if he could wash away his doubts and fears and loneliness in her. Willow didn't shy away but kissed him back just as hard, holding him tightly to her, and for the first time he could remember, Logan didn't feel alone.

CHAPTER TEN

WILLOW PICKED UP her bag, testing the weight. Maybe she had overpacked, but what did one take away for a long weekend boating? This wasn't the slow traversing of a canal she'd grown up with but actual ocean sailing. To her relief, her lack of actual experience with sails and masts wasn't a problem—although Logan's boat looked pretty luxurious and spacious to her, he had bought it to be able to sail one-handed when needed. Not that it was his racing boat. That small, spartan and expensive piece of kit was still in California.

She couldn't deny she was excited about the trip. Partly it was the prospect of a couple of days off thanks to the Memorial Day long weekend, partly the opportunity to explore a little more of her temporary home with a route taking in Salem and Cape Cod planned. But mixed in with that excitement was a little trepidation. She and Logan would be spending the extended weekend together, just the two of them.

The weeks since their meal at The Harbour Inn and resulting love-making had kept a similar pattern to the ones before, only now they shared a bed nearly every night and spent most Fridays at The Harbour Inn with Logan's family. It was obvious to Willow how much his uncle and aunt loved Logan, and his relationship with Nate reminded her of Skye and her, best friends and family combined. It was painful to realise he couldn't take the love for granted, that their kindness and love didn't make up for his own father's contempt and rejection. Not that they had returned to the confidences of that first night and morning on the boat. Logan had been his usual charming, insouciant self since then, his barriers once more firmly up. It was probably for the best. That barrier kept the sex fun and fulfilling but stripped away some of the devastating intimacy that had made it harder to keep her heart intact.

In some ways, Logan was exactly what she needed. He was successful in his own right, financially secure, gave her all the independence she wanted. There was safety in his name, in his wealth. And there was the connection between them, an understanding that had sprung up from the moment he had pulled her back from the kerbside. But he was emotionally unavailable in ways she knew would only grow. She had thought that kind of closeness was an optional extra in a life partner, but now she was living with it, she knew she would rather be alone than glorified housemates with benefits, however good those benefits were and however congenial the housemate.

Besides, even if she was prepared to live in a perpetual half marriage—always considering he wanted to, of course—there was still the memory of Vegas taunting her. The memory of twenty hours of hedonism including the ceremony that had brought her here. Logan might be working sixteen-hour days, but he was still the adrenaline junkie who had brought out the side of her she had spent her life suppressing. Much safer to say goodbye at the end of the year as planned.

So, although she was more than happy to share her time, companionship and body with him, her heart had to remain out of reach.

Her watch vibrated with a message, and when Willow checked her phone, she saw a brief text from Logan to say he had been held up at Lona and would meet her at the boat in an hour. Willow looked around her room.

Her laptop was closed and her out-of-office on, her bag packed. Logan's father was out golfing, not that she had reached the point of making polite conversation with him yet anyway. She wasn't sure she ever would.

Her window overlooked the beach nearest the town, and as she gazed out at the receding tide and the people enjoying the beach in anticipation of the long weekend, a building in the distance snagged her interest. Romney was a small town, with every part walkable including the small industrial area the other side of the harbour where Lona had its headquarters. Why not meet Logan there?

Activity was always more interesting than waiting around. Decision made, Willow grabbed her bag and made her way out of the apartment and down the staircase, popping her head into the kitchen to say goodbye to Brigid, the housekeeper, and wish her a nice long weekend.

As usual, she decided to leave the grounds by the gate leading onto the beach rather than head down the drive and onto the road, and soon found herself on the sea side of the dunes. How things had changed in three months. When she'd moved here, she could usually be guaranteed to have the beach to herself apart from a few distant dog walkers at most times of the day, but it had been getting busier and busier as summer approached. Now, with a holiday weekend ahead, it was more crowded than she had ever seen it. The Sea Shack was doing a roaring trade as she passed it, and so she didn't stop, raising her hand to Lou, busy at the counter, in greeting instead. In some ways it was nice to see the town come alive, but part of her missed the peace and solitude.

Her bag got heavier as she neared the harbour, and she was glad when she reached the Inn and quickly popped in to leave it behind the bar to collect on her way back, feeling extra light and full of anticipation as she carried on along the road. This was all uncharted territory, the ocean behind her as she turned into the business park.

The Lona factory and headquarters were housed in a ten-year-old eco building, created to be as sustainable as the boards and accessories manufactured inside, from the grass roof and solar panels to the recycled interiors. Willow had read all about it but not yet seen it in person. She looked around in interest as she reached the reception area and pushed the door beyond open, finding herself in a comfortable office painted in a friendly sea blue, desks at one end, a large table and chairs at the other, with sofas grouped around coffee tables in the middle. It was very different from the formality of the HartCo head office.

Clearly most of the office staff had headed off to start their weekend early, but a couple of people looked up when she entered, and a woman of around Willow's age got to her feet with a friendly smile. 'Can I help?'

'Hi, I'm looking for Logan.' She paused. 'I'm Willow.'

The other woman's eyes widened. She obviously knew exactly who Willow was. 'Oh, hi. I'm Jen, the social media manager. Lovely to meet you at last. Logan is just in the factory. Come with me.'

Willow followed Jen through a wood-clad corridor and up a flight of stairs leading to a gallery running around a double-height room. More stairs led onto the factory floor at intervals. Doors studded along both walls led into unseen rooms. Peeking over the railings, she could see various machines, and boards in various stages of manufacture.

'Have you been here before?' Jen asked, and Willow shook her head.

'I've not had a chance. It's all very impressive.'

'I'll let Logan do the grand tour, but this is where we make the cheaper and entry-level mass-produced boards. The next room is for bespoke and handmade, the room beyond for wetsuits, and storage beyond that. This gallery runs the length of the building to make sure we don't traipse all over the factory floor and create a health and safety risk. There are meeting rooms off here and some more offices.'

'There's what? Eighty people employed here?'

'About that. Some of our manufacturing is off-site, clothing and accessories and things like that, but any subcontractors have to meet our strict eco and employer standards. But you know all this, of course.'

'Of course,' Willow agreed, and she did, but only through reading the website. Logan didn't talk much about Lona when they were alone, apart from a few stories about its founding and some discussions about the search for the right leadership team to take over from him and Nate. She knew it was an impressive company, but being here in this statement of a building and actually seeing people at work, it struck her anew just what Logan was giving up to fulfil his family obligations. He seemed reconciled to his future, was insightful and impressive when she saw him in meetings, but the very nature of HartCo meant he would always be tucked away on the executive floor reading reports, not being so hands-on and doing stuff. Here he could do both.

She asked a few questions as she followed Jen along the gallery corridor until they reached the third manufacturing room, where she saw Logan standing by a display dummy that was wearing a wetsuit. He was deep in conversation with a couple of young men, neither of whom looked old enough to be out of school.

'That's our newest product, the most eco-friendly wetsuit on the market,' Jen said proudly. 'We're planning to launch it for the new season. We're just doing the last checks now. It's not good enough for it just to be the best environmentally. It has to perform as well as any of its competitors too.'

'Of course.' At that moment, Logan looked up and noticed them, holding up his hand in a greeting. She returned the gesture, half-shy. 'Who are those boys? Are they on work experience?'

'In a way. Jake is on our high school diploma scheme, Kegan the rehabilitation scheme. They've both made quite an impression. I would be surprised if they weren't offered permanent positions.'

'Of course.' Willow didn't want to admit she didn't know what Jen was talking about.

It didn't take Logan long to finish his conversation and climb the open staircase up to the gallery. 'Willow, what are you doing here?' He kissed her, brief but affectionate, and Willow was aware of Jen watching them. She was sure Logan's sudden marriage must have caused a fair share of office gossip, and nice as Jen seemed, it was likely she would share every moment of Willow's visit with her colleagues. It all felt more intimate than HartCo, where she was somewhat protected from staff curiosity by her new elevated status.

'I was all packed, and so thought I'd come and meet you here.' Logan had taken his bag with him when he'd left a few hours before. 'I hope that's okay.'

'Of course. It's a nice surprise. Has Jen given you the tour?'

'I made a start,' Jen said. 'Lovely to meet you, Willow. I'd better get back. There's a lot to do before I clock off.'

Willow returned her smile. 'Thank you for the tour. It was lovely to meet you too.'

'Okay then.' Logan took her hand. 'Come see my company.'

'I don't want to interrupt if there's anything you should be doing.'

'No, I'm done. I just needed to see Jake and Kegan before they finished for the weekend. Okay, come this way.'

'Jen mentioned they were on some kind of work experience scheme,' Willow said as she followed him downstairs onto the factory floor. It was light, thanks to huge skylights in the roof far above them, the slightly tinted glass ensuring it wasn't too warm.

'That's right, we run two right now, both for young people, although I'd like to extend them to older people as well. The first is for young people in danger of dropping out without a high school diploma, especially if they need to repeat a year. We offer paid part-time work with assignments that can count towards credits if they stay in school and a guaranteed year's work experience after graduation. The second is a day release scheme for young offenders. Similar lines with the opportunity to apply for jobs after release.'

'That's incredible. You must make such a difference.'

'Small-scale, but I sit on the board of a charity working with other small and medium local employers to help them offer the same, so it all adds up to enough second chances to hopefully turn some lives around.'

'You are a very surprising man, Logan Prestwood Hartwell. Just when I think I've got the hang of you, I discover something more.'

'I like to keep my wife on her toes. Come on, we've just got some new samples through for next year's designs. Let's find you something for the weekend.'

'Living the brand on our trip?' she teased, and he smiled as he leaned in to kiss her.

'Always.'

Logan stretched out on the built-in cushioned sun lounger and stared up at the stars, Willow lying by his side, her hands clasped over her stomach, so still she seemed asleep.

'I like Salem,' she said after a while. 'I'd like to explore more, but I'm excited for the Cape too.'

'We can come back to explore any time. It's only a half hour drive from Romney. I think you're going to like Wellfleet too. It's on the sheltered side of the Cape, so if it stays this warm, you might be able to swim even this early in the season. Just look out for the great whites.'

'Will you think me very unadventurous if

I say I'm a bit apprehensive about swimming with sharks?'

He laughed. 'Just steer clear of the seals and you should be okay. The shallow bay side beaches are usually fine, and it's too early in the season to swim in the oceanside ones for all but the hardiest of swimmers. They beaches are good for surfers but pretty chilly still.'

'I should have chosen a wetsuit rather than a swimsuit.'

'Next time. Then I can give you a surf lesson. The sailing ones seem to have gone okay.'

'But I know my way around a boat, even if it's a very different style. Ropes and knots and tillers are in my DNA, but a surfboard is very much not. Maybe I am too old to learn.'

'Not even close. Put it on that to-do list of yours and then failure won't be an option.'

'You know me too well.'

The words hung there. They were true. He did know her despite both their efforts to keep their emotional distance. She was under his skin, in his blood. 'I've never brought a girl-friend aboard before,' he said before he could remember all the reasons it would be a bad idea.

Her shift was so subtle, he wouldn't have

felt it if he wasn't so closely attuned to her every move.

'Why not?'

'The sea is where I come to escape.'

'And you need to escape your relationships?'

'More that I didn't want anyone to get too close.'

'But here I am.'

'Ah, but you're my wife.' He couldn't say why that made a difference. He just knew it did. But it was more than that. It was because she was Willow.

'Do you remember back on the beach when you asked me why I said yes to marrying you?'

'I do.'

'And I wanted to know why you asked me in the first place.'

'You did.'

'You said it felt right.'

'I did.'

'What did you mean?'

Clearly two-syllable answers weren't going to help him here.

'I can't explain it,' he said helplessly. 'The rest of that day makes perfect sense. There you were, a little shook up, feeling some regret for wasted opportunities. I'd played the perfect son and heir that week for long enough. I wanted to have some fun, had already planned to do so, and liked the idea of company. You were beautiful, but more, I felt connected to you. I liked watching you try new things—I'll never forget your face when you finished the zip line. You looked so wild, so proud of yourself. I didn't propose the challenges with the end goal of sleeping with you, but as the day went on, it seemed inevitable that we would end up in bed.'

'I know. Until I told you I didn't do one-night stands.'

'Nor do I. But nor do I marry women I've known for less than twenty-four hours. It was something about the wistful way you said you thought eloping was romantic. It was something I could give you. A way of keeping that connection.' He had wanted to keep challenging her, delighting in her reaction, her response. He had wanted to sleep with her, to give her something no one else had. Well, he'd got his wish, but at what cost?

Only three months in and he was getting far too used to having her around.

'Do you regret it?'

He thought carefully. 'I regret disrupting your life.'

Willow reached over and ran a finger down his cheek, his neck, before letting her hand rest on his chest. 'I was there, Logan. I had agency.'

Logan leaned over and kissed her, still unable to believe that it could be this easy, that he and Willow could be this comfortable together, to have found a way of enjoying this time together with no hard feelings. But as he deepened the kiss, ran one hand down to cup her hip, pushing the material of her dress up until he was circling warm skin, his other hand tangled in the silk of her hair, he was aware he was being dishonest with them both. He didn't have any regrets yet, but he would. That day of reckoning was still far away, but every day brought it nearer. He was getting too used to having her around, questioning, pushing, making him think and feel and come to terms with the cards he'd been dealt. But she was borrowed. She had a life and family far away from here. This time next year, he would have handed over control of his company to someone else and given Willow her freedom. Then what would he have? Who would he be?

But that was then, and this was now, and she was gloriously warm under him, soft in all the right places, her hands sure and knowing as she touched him in turn. 'Come on,' he said, reluctantly pulling away. 'Let's go below. This is a little too exposed.'

'What did you have in mind when we get there?'

'Whatever my lady wants,' he promised, and was rewarded by her slow smile.

'In that case,' she said, 'what are we waiting for?'

Hold on to this moment, Logan told himself as he slid to his feet and extended a hand to help Willow up. He bent to kiss her, and her hands entwined around his neck. *Hold on to it. This is happiness. Remember it.*

CHAPTER ELEVEN

'ARE YOU SURE I look okay?' Willow twisted to look at herself in the mirror, unsure of the stranger she saw there. The pale green full-length sheath was beautiful, the designer shoes surprisingly comfortable for such delicate scraps of leather. She wore diamonds in her ears and around her neck, mollified when she'd found out they were family heirlooms she could leave behind when she finally went home and not an extravagant gift. Her hair had been professionally put up into a deceptively simple knot, her make-up done to emphasise the hollows of her cheeks, to bring out the green in her hazel eyes. She looked beautiful, alien, other. She looked glowing, rich. She looked like the wife of Logan Prestwood Hartwell III.

'You look more than okay.' Logan's sharp intake of breath was all she needed. 'Almost too good to touch.'

'That's the problem with being all dressed up.'

'True. We could sneak away. You in a bikini, me in shorts, the boat…' She had no idea if he was serious or not, but she couldn't deny that she was tempted.

'Your father is expecting us, and he is hosting…'

'Details, details…'

'Come on, Logan, let's get down there before I lose my nerve.'

Logan held out an arm, as if they were heading to a Regency ball. 'Promise me every dance.'

'Isn't that rude?'

'We're newlyweds. It's expected.'

'We'll see. Right. Let's do this.' Willow straightened her spine, not wanting Logan to sense how nervous she really was. She'd soon realised that the Hartwell Fourth of July garden party was no mere gathering of friends but a much looked forward to institution on the society calendar. It started early evening with an al fresco dinner, charity auction and entertainment, followed by a prime view of the town fireworks, which were set off out at sea. The rarely used ballroom was then opened up for dancing, with a barbecue at midnight. The whole evening was ostensibly a fundraising event, but Logan assured her the real purpose was to see and be seen. And this year, invites were more sought after than usual as this was Willow's introduction to society—and society's introduction to her.

Willow could feel nervous giggles bubbling up inside as she and Logan descended the sweeping staircase—slowly, the heels wouldn't allow for anything else—to a sea of upturned heads. It seemed half the guests had already arrived and were waiting for their first glimpse of the Hartwell bride. She felt as if she were in a historical movie or novel, the silk of her dress brushing against her calves, diamonds in her ears and at her throat. It was all so absurd—and mortifying. Worse than her first day on the executive floor, being stared at and judged on appearance alone. Any friendly face she did recognise belonged to townsfolk drafted in to work for the day. She was grateful for Logan's arm, calm and steady where her hand rested. When she stole a glance at him, his face expressed nothing but relaxed welcome, but she could sense the tension in his shoulders. This world was his world, had been his childhood, his young adulthood. No wonder he had escaped to the freedom of the ocean whenever he could.

Logan's father waited at the bottom of the

stairs and took her hand from Logan as if she were a prized possession ready to be shown off. And in some ways, she was. Willow was only just realising how many calculations she had upset when her marriage to Logan had been announced. The guest list was full of old and rich East Coast families, many of whom had hoped to marry their daughters into the Hartwell dynasty.

Well, next year they could make their play. It was likely Logan would accept his fate. He knew he needed children if HartCo was to continue as it had for generations. The whole business was feudal, ridiculous really, but also understandable on many levels. She couldn't disrupt what had to be for too long. She just hoped he chose someone kind. He deserved kindness, needed it more than he would ever admit.

Logan's father hailed an older man with a gleaming smile and improbable head of hair. 'John, let me introduce you to my beautiful and talented daughter-in-law.' Willow sucked in a breath to quell her nervously squirming stomach and summoned up a matching smile to the one Logan was employing as he greeted an older couple flanked by two teenage daughters. It was time to host.

It was an exhausting evening. Willow lost

count of how many people she spoke to, mechanically recycling the same answers to the same questions. Yes, she had met Logan at work; yes, they'd eloped; yes, it was terribly romantic; yes, she had settled in at Lookout House; yes, she was very much enjoying living in New England. Yes, she was English… yes, she had lived in London. No, she hadn't met the Queen. It was a relief when the fireworks began and conversation ceased for twenty minutes during the spectacular show. She'd managed to find Logan just before the fireworks began and watched the sky light up in myriad colours from within the safety of his arms. Every now and then she could feel his lips brush her hair, her ear, the side of her neck. Onlookers smiled indulgently. They were honeymooners, after all, and right now she was prepared to indulge the fantasy.

She didn't quite manage to fulfil her promise to dance every dance with Logan. Manners dictated that she grant one dance to her father-in-law, and several guests asked her as well. Despite her protestations that she had no idea what she was doing, she managed to acquit herself well enough not to feel like she had made herself a laughing stock. The room had been transformed. Usually there was something a little sad about the ballroom, with its vast expanse of empty wooden floor, the row of closed French doors, glimpses of the terrace beyond, a relic of a time long before. But tonight it was lit to resemble candlelight, the doors flung open to the summer night, the terraces hung with fairy lights. Tables and chairs were dotted around so partygoers could rest between dances. A small classical band had started the dancing off with waltzes and polkas. They were now replaced by a cover band playing popular songs from across the last five decades. Bars had been set up in the adjoining ante room and outside. Wait staff circulated with trays of drinks and more canapés whilst at the end of the terrace, the grills had been lit, ready to cook the midnight feast. It was extravagant and over the top. It was Logan's world.

Despite everything, Willow realised she'd not really appreciated just how different their worlds were until now. The house, the global business, the staff, the black credit card, the boats, the designer wardrobe, the chauffeur-driven car had all started to seem normal. This evening was a wake-up call. She didn't belong here, in a world where the talk swung between stocks and scandal, gossip and tennis dates, where everyone knew each other as had their parents and grandparents before them, where every accessory cost more than she would usually spend on a full outfit. A closed society of money, lineage and customs.

And for all her fine feathers, she belonged on the outside.

She held on to Logan a little tighter, glad he was there to anchor her in this strange world.

He smiled down at her. 'You okay?'

'Of course,' she said automatically before honesty compelled her to add, 'A little overwhelmed maybe. There are a lot of people here.'

'You were quite the draw. My father will be preening himself. This will be the highlight of the summer. Of course he will only talk about how much we raised, as if that was the purpose of the evening.'

'It wasn't?' The charity auction had been eye-opening, with staggering amounts bid for uses of holiday homes by people who already owned two or three of their own, private chefs, tennis lessons by Wimbledon champions, signed memorabilia, VIP packages to concerts and plays and operas. Willow had quickly understood that it wasn't necessarily the items themselves the bidders were bidding for. The purpose was to be seen conspicuously spending money, to show how altruistic they were.

'It's a good excuse. Gets him into the papers, the society pages, a reminder of our centuries of wealth and power and philanthropy.'

'Will you continue with the annual party? When you're head of the family?'

'There was a time when I would have said absolutely not,' Logan admitted. 'But it *is* tradition, and whatever the reasons for bidding, it raises a lot of money. Hopefully it's not something I will have to worry about for a long time.' He looked searchingly into her eyes. 'Come on, let's get you out of here. You look like you need a break.'

Willow didn't demur. She was tired, she realised, not so much because of the late hour or the dancing or from being on her feet for most of the evening but from constantly making small talk, making sure she said the right thing, not just maintaining the fiction of the newly wed, madly-in-love couple but also Willow Jones, respectable financial director, not the home-educated child of hippy parents. To this crowd, an alternative lifestyle was refusing Botox. She wanted to fit in for Logan's sake. She didn't want news of their split to be met with a chorus of *I told you so*.

Logan didn't take her out through the terrace and crowds. Instead he wove a route through the house, bypassing anyone they might need to stop and talk to. 'Thank you,' Willow said as they slipped through the kitchen, the usually tranquil space unrecognisable now, filled with catering equipment and staff. 'I needed this.'

From the kitchen door, it was less than five minutes to the discreet gate which led directly onto the beach. Willow stopped to remove her shoes partway, tucking them into the summer house for safety, relishing the coolness of the grass against her tired bare soles and then the softness of sand between her toes.

The beach had been crammed earlier with picnickers and families watching the fireworks. Now just groups of mainly young people were left, many sitting round driftwood fires. Scents of roasted marshmallows mingled with the smoke and the salt of the sea, and Willow breathed it in. 'It's not that I wasn't having a nice time, but I feel like I belong on this side of the fence. I'd be just as happy, happier, sitting around one of those fires than with all that rich food and small talk.' She recollected her audience and winced. 'That sounds very ungrateful, especially as everyone was so kind. I'm sorry.'

'Not at all. When I was younger, I would frequently escape to do just that. I could build you a fire if you wanted?'

She laughed. 'I couldn't sit on the sand in this dress, but thank you. I'm happy just to walk.'

They meandered along the beach for a little while, heading away from the mansion and the town. There were fewer people around the further away they walked, and Willow breathed deeply, letting the air, the sound of the sea, the peace replenish her soul. 'I'm going to miss this when I'm back in London. Waking up to see the ocean in all its moods is just a joy. Dawn or midnight, sun, storms, mist, I love it all.'

'Yes.' Logan sounded thoughtful and then lapsed into silence. Willow made a few more comments as they continued to walk, but he barely grunted in response. After a while she stopped trying, enjoying the peace and air until Logan finally spoke. 'There's no reason for you to miss it. The ocean, I mean. Miss Romney or living here. After all, I chose a year as an end point because it seemed a sensible amount of time, long enough to make the marriage seem more than a whim, short enough to not impact on either of our lives too much. But it's not set in stone. We could extend it. If you wanted. For as long as it feels right.'

Willow stopped. It was so dark she could

barely make out his features, and his tone gave away no hint as to his feelings. The thud of her pulse began to drown out the roar of the incoming tide. Did she *want* to stay here indefinitely? And if so, why? She could, of course, move to live by the sea. If she kept her position at HartCo, she could even stay in Massachusetts if she chose. But that wasn't what he was suggesting. He was suggesting she stay with him. Stay married to him. But this time with no agreed end date.

Which made it less of an agreed marriage and more of an actual marriage.

Turning away from Logan to look out at the moonlit sea, Willow tried to envision what that meant. It meant a continuation of all the things that made her happy, their Friday nights at the Inn, the companionable commute into the city on the train, coffee on the table between them, Logan on his laptop, she gazing out of the window. It meant more weekends sailing around the coast, the chance to enjoy promised trips to explore further afield, winter and snow as she had never seen it, complete with winter sports. Not just for one calendar cycle, not a year out, but a lifestyle.

It meant spending night after night together. Willow closed her eyes and held her arms out, feeling the night breeze dance on her skin. No saying goodbye to all-consuming kisses, to sure, sweet caresses, to desiring and feeling desired. 'How long are you thinking?'

Two years? Three? Five? Forever?

'Like I said, as long as it feels right. Until either of us wanted out.'

Logan still sounded almost offhand, as if this was no more important than discussing weekend plans. Her stomach twisted, her chest tightening as an inescapable feeling of dread crept over her. Whatever she decided, everything was about to change. 'Why mention it now?' she asked at last. 'We're only four months into the year, after all. You might change your mind by autumn, be fed up with me by then. Don't make offers you might regret.' She attempted a laugh, but it fell flat. She curled her fingers into fists, almost glad of the sharpness of her nails in her palms.

'You said it yourself, you love it here. I wanted you to know you had options. That this can be your home for as long as you want. You don't have to leave until you're ready to.'

The monotone of his voice bore into her, and her fists tightened. Was it really so casual an offer to him? Her decision not mattering either way? Didn't she matter? 'What do you want? Do you *want* me to stay?'

'Of course.' Now he just sounded surprised as if she should have known that all along. 'We work well together, Willow. You fit in here. My father likes you. Nate, my uncle and aunt, they like you. I like being with you, whether that's here or in bed. I'll be honest, what we have here is more than I actually expected from marriage. What's the point of throwing this away to marry someone else, someone with whom I might not get on so well, when we are already married and it works?'

Sucking in her breath, Willow tried to consider his point fairly. She had to concede he was making some kind of sense. They did get on, as friends as well as lovers. Why walk away when they might not ever meet anyone else with whom they were so compatible? Her fears that he might tempt her into behaving recklessly had proved unfounded. The Logan of the last four months had been hardworking, sober, respectable, all qualities she valued.

It was churlish to admit that she kind of missed the dangerous smile and daredevil glint of the Logan she had first met. The way that Logan had pushed and challenged her to be more. This Logan was allowing her to settle.

Willow tried to turn his proposal over dispassionately despite the nagging feeling that there was something very wrong here. Was liking enough? She wasn't naive. She knew there were no guarantees in marriage, in any relationship, that even people who started out head over heels in love could find themselves divorced with no idea how they got there. But at least they started out with hope.

She turned to Logan, still with no idea what she thought, how she wanted to respond. Then she remembered standing by the roulette table, chips in hand, Logan standing behind her, her whole body already attuned to his every move and his words, words she had repeated back to him just a few weeks before.

The key to gambling, whether it's money or business, is to know what you are willing to lose and stop there.

Was she willing to gamble any more of her heart to Logan?

Her *heart*? Where had that come from? Her body, yes. Her emotions, yes, but her heart? Surely she had kept that safe? But what was this aching sense of loss? This feeling of having been handed everything she wanted, only for it to not be enough? This misery engulfing her, a physical pain in her chest, her throat, burning her eyes? And then she knew. It was too late. She had gambled and she had lost. At some point over the last four months, she had fallen in love with her husband, a man who was now offering her everything she could want, except loving her back.

It wasn't like Logan to rush his fences, and he knew he had here. Willow was right. They had two thirds of their agreed year to go. Why mention an extension now?

'Look, Willow. You don't have to decide now. I'm just saying the offer is there if you want it.' But he couldn't help but realise that her surprise, her hesitation hurt in a way he hadn't expected. He thought she liked him, the life they were slowly building. That she might see the benefits of his suggestion.

'What about love?'

Willow's voice was so low, Logan didn't hear her at first, but as he took in her words, he could feel his body almost physically recoil, the blood hammering around his body in panic. 'Love doesn't come with any guarantee of happiness. You know that. You said yourself you want security, financial and emotional security. I can give you that, Willow.'

'How secure is it if either of us can just walk away when we want to?'

'Love doesn't prevent that.' He swallowed. He could feel her slipping away with every word, his chest, his very soul aching with an indescribable sense of impending loss. 'Look, we know what we're getting here. We respect one another. We're compatible. That counts for more than love.'

'So you *don't* love me?'

Do you love me?

The thought shocked him, and he pushed it away. He didn't seek love. He wasn't that foolish.

He tried for a laugh, the panic increasing, roaring in his ears. 'What *is* love, Willow? I like you, I want you, I enjoy being with you. I respect you. Isn't that enough? Look, don't make a big deal of this, Willow. You can say no, with no hard feelings, and we carry on as we are.'

But even as he said the words, he knew they weren't true. The proposition was out there. He'd made himself vulnerable, shown himself as needy, ruined a good thing by wanting more. Stupid. Greedy. Foolish boy.

Willow took a while to answer, and when she did, her voice was still low, thick, as though fighting back tears. 'Thank you for the offer.

I really appreciate it, but I think I need more. No. I *know* I need more. I deserve more. I deserve love, Logan. To give it and to receive it, and I would rather be alone than settle. Do you understand?'

All too well. Of course a woman like Willow deserved more. Why should she settle for the little his stunted heart could offer? 'Of course. It was just a thought. Like I said, no hard feelings.'

'But it's more than that. Even if I could settle, I wouldn't want to do that to you. You deserve more too,' she went on relentlessly. 'You're a really good man, Logan. You are kind and generous and worthy of love and loving. You just need to believe that. I wish I could help you believe that.'

To his horror, Logan could feel his throat start to swell, his eyes sting. He hadn't cried in twenty-five years. He wasn't going to start now. 'Willow,' he drawled in as offhand a manner as he could manage. 'Come on, let's not go all movie-of-the-week here now. We have a good laugh, and the sex is amazing. Selfishly I don't want to give that up, but if that's not enough for you, then we're good. Nothing's changed. Come on, let's get back to the party.'

'Yes. Of course.' She didn't say any more,

but as they made their way back, now not touching or speaking, he knew he was wrong. Things *had* changed, and they were never going to be right again.

CHAPTER TWELVE

IT HAD BEEN an exhausting week. For all their attempts to pretend that everything was normal, Willow knew she and Logan were failing miserably. She still shared a bed with him, but there was something desperate, something frantic in their love-making, and afterwards they slept so far apart, the middle of the bed felt like a chasm. The companionship, the fun had gone.

She'd hurt him desperately, she knew. Part of her wanted to tell him why she couldn't accept his offer, why it wasn't enough, but she shrank from making herself so vulnerable. Knowing Logan thought himself incapable of loving or being loved physically pained her, but the memory of his mocking tone on the beach kept her silent; she couldn't face the thought of his pity, his rejection if she spoke up.

And he didn't love her. He liked her, he desired her, he wanted her, but he didn't love her. Love had never been part of their deal. She knew that, but she had opened her heart to him, and he had brushed her honesty, her feelings away as if they were nothing. She couldn't allow herself to think about it, to feel it, because if she did, she wasn't sure she could carry on.

Even so, she had no idea how they could limp on like this for another eight months.

Over the last week, Willow had elected to go into the office every day while Logan worked from home or the Lona offices. She felt relieved by the time away from him, only seeing him in occasional virtual meetings. She returned late after a hurried meal at her desk, glad of the excuse her ever-increasing workload gave her. Tonight, even though it was Friday, she had stayed later than ever, and it was after ten by the time she had walked the short distance from the train station to the house and made her way up to their apartment.

The lights were off and the apartment in darkness when she got in, and she was conscious of equal amounts of relief and disappointment when she found herself alone. Logan had probably gone to The Harbour Inn. Maybe she could be asleep when he returned. But the weekend still loomed ahead of them, and she realised with a sinking heart this couldn't go on. They were going to have to sort this out. She just had no idea how. Relieved to have come to some kind of decision, Willow dropped her bag onto the hallway floor and switched on the lamp to see an envelope illuminated on the hallway table, her name handwritten on it.

Her heart began to pound, her hands sweaty as she picked it up. She took it into the sitting room, where she sat down before opening it. The solidity of the envelope felt ominous, final somehow. She opened it carefully and peered inside to see several pieces of paper and a set of keys. She left the keys for now, drawing out the papers and sorting through them mechanically. The first was the deed to her sister's building, in her name. The second was an estate agent's brochure. Her eyes ached as she took it in, detailing the particulars for one of the cottages by the canal she had told Logan about. Her tears fell thickly even as she tried to hold them back. The third item was a plane ticket in her name to London, two days from now. It was a single, she noted with a stab of pain, not a return. The fourth, finally, a letter. She blinked furiously, trying to clear her eyes so she could read it.

Dear Willow,

It was unfair of me to drag you into my family dramas. I should have found another way to protect you, so I'm doing what I should have done at the start and freeing you of any obligation with sincere thanks for all you have done.

As the one to renege on the deal, it seems only fair I give the building to you anyway. I hope your sister and her family will be happy there. I have also bought you a bonus and beg you to accept it. We should all achieve our dreams every once in a while, and if you can't live by the ocean, you should still look out at water. It will make me very happy to think of you there.

I've flown to California to interview a possible new CEO for Lona and drive my competition boat back—I won't be back until the middle of next week, so you can leave without any awkwardness. I've told my father you have a family emergency back in London, and when I get back, I'll tell him the truth. Don't worry about your job. It won't be hard for me to take all the blame. He adores you. So do I.

I hope the man you deserve is out

there and that when you find him, he loves you the way I can't.

L

'Oh, the stupid, stubborn fool.' Willow set the .letter down beside her, giving up the battle and letting the tears flow freely. 'I understand now.'

And she did. Logan was so scared of rejection, of commitment, of being found wanting, he had pushed her away before she left him. Yet he had done so in a way that made it hardest for her to leave. 'He bought me my cottage,' she whispered, touching the brochure with reverent fingers. From the flower-filled front garden to the blue front door, the views from the bedroom over the canal to the bench at the front, it was exactly what she had dreamed of.

But she would be living there alone.

'I need time to think,' she said aloud, her brain whirling with a myriad of mixed emotions and thoughts. Logan had broken her heart whilst making her dreams come true. He was giving her sister a lifetime of security and condemning Willow to loneliness. He had remembered what she had told him and planned this for her.

She wiped away her tears as she made herself push emotion aside and consider the facts. Consider the sentiment and knowledge and sacrifice in his actions. He had tried to make her dreams come true by taking all responsibility for their marriage and split on himself, ensuring there would never be the understanding with his father she knew he craved. These weren't the actions or the letter of a man who didn't know how to love. For the first time in the long week, hope flared. There were no sureties in life or love, but Willow couldn't believe that a man who remembered her childhood dream and enabled it was acting purely out of guilt.

'I'm a coward,' she said sternly to herself as she held the brochure tight, and with the word came a tidal wave of relief. 'I was too scared to tell him exactly how I felt because I couldn't face rejection, but that's exactly what he needs to hear. Hints aren't enough, not for Logan. He needs to *know* how I feel. I need to show him.'

But the question she couldn't answer was how. She needed time and space to figure it out. She needed her family.

It was hot in London, the sticky heat of the city in summer, and even though the tem-

perature was lower than the one she'd left behind, it felt more uncomfortable. Her adored
city seemed louder than ever, too big as the
taxi drove through endless streets until they
reached her neighbourhood. She found herself longing for Boston with its green spaces
and wide streets. The journey took her past
her flat, currently rented out to a friend of
Skye's. Looking at the bland building, she
felt as if a lifetime had gone by since she had
last occupied the top corner. Finally the taxi
pulled into the road leading onto the canal.
Willow got out, case in hand, and paid the
driver. She was bone tired despite sleeping
throughout the flight thanks to the first-class
seat Logan had booked for her, but despite
that, despite everything, a tingle of excitement swirled through her as she felt for her
keys. The excitement and anticipation stayed
with her as she walked along the canal and
then opened the iron gate to set foot into *her*
front garden. She walked down the stone path
to open the front door.

A quick online shop a couple of days ago
and a call to Skye meant that instead of walking into an empty house, she walked into a
sparsely furnished one. A two-seater sofa
and coffee table occupied the small sitting
room, but the built-in bookshelves were bare,

as was the mantelpiece above the fireplace. There was a table with four chairs in the kitchen/diner, and when Willow opened the cupboards, she found a dinner set with four plates, bowls and mugs in one, tea bags— proper English tea, she thought ecstatically— and coffee in another, along with a loaf of bread. The new fridge was set in place, and inside were milk, butter, cheese and some cherry tomatoes. Willow carried her bag up to the front bedroom, which held a bed, already made up. There were towels in the bathroom. It wasn't much but more than adequate for her needs. If things went the way she wanted them to, then this would be a pied-à-terre for when she visited her family. If not, well, she had the rest of her life to furnish it.

A quick shower and one perfect cup of tea later and Willow was once more locking the door, taking a moment to take in the view, to look at the abundance of summer flowers in the small but pretty garden. She smiled ruefully as she touched a pink cabbage rose. This was the garden of her dreams. Logan had chosen well. She set off towards Skye's, almost jogging despite the heat of the day, desperate to see her sister and to get her wise advice, the deed to the building tucked securely in her bag. The time for lies and subterfuge was over. She would tell her sister everything, and this time she wouldn't try and figure it all out on her own.

Logan had never minded long road trips before, but the four days it took him to drive from California to Romney were the longest and loneliest of his life. In this mood, he needed distraction, adrenaline, not the torture of being left alone with his thoughts. And they were torture. There was no getting away from the realisation that he was a coward, no better than his father, using money to try and solve problems of his own making.

He'd half hoped Willow would call, even if it was to shout at him but his phone had stayed stubbornly silent, his only nonwork messages from Nate.

She was probably glad to leave, glad to be shot of him. And he was supposed to be glad she had gone, filled with the righteous glow of having done the right thing. But he wasn't. He just felt flat, as if there was no hope or joy anywhere. As if there never could be again.

It was evening by the time he had dropped the boat off at the yard for a check. Logan had entered into a race from Boston in a week's time and knew he was out of practice, but even as he arranged a time to take the boat out the following day, he couldn't feel any enthusiasm for the challenge. He drove slowly through the tourist-filled streets, past children with ice creams and youths with body boards and young couples holding hands, hoping to see a slim straight-backed young woman with light brown hair and a smile that lit up the world around her, but she wasn't there. And as soon as he set foot in Lookout House, he knew she wasn't there, either.

Logan didn't wait for his father's summons, not this time. Instead he made his way straight to the study and then, when he couldn't find his father there, outside to find his dad standing by a rose bush and looking out to sea, his expression as inscrutable as ever.

'Dad, there's something I need to tell you.' Straight in, there would be no prevarication.

But his father just looked at him. 'I know, son.' That *son* was like a sucker punch to his stomach, as was the sadness in his father's voice. 'Willow told me everything.'

'She's gone, hasn't she? Oh, Dad. What am I going to do?'

Logan sank to his knees by his father's side and buried his head in his hands. Tears would be a relief, but he had spent a lifetime fighting them back, and his body couldn't give in

him now. Instead desolation and despair tore
through him, a double tornado of agony, and
one of his own making. After a while he felt
a heavy hand on his head. 'Come on, let's
get a drink.'

It was an evening full of surprises. Logan's father hadn't meant, as Logan expected,
a drink at the house. Instead the two men
walked down to The Harbour Inn. Logan
couldn't remember his father ever having
set foot in there during his lifetime, and the
older man hesitated at the door, his eyes dark
with memories. 'It's been a long time,' he
murmured.

It seemed that they were expected. A private table was reserved, set away from the
public spaces. They ordered drinks, and Connor himself brought them over, including one
for himself. He pulled out a chair and joined
them.

'Hartwell,' he said curtly to his brother-
in-law.

Logan's father inclined his head. 'Good to
see you, Connor. Thanks for accommodating
us.' The history between the two hung there,
thick, palpable, almost visible. It was almost
a relief when Connor turned to Logan.

'Let's have it. What scrape have you got
yourself into this time?' There was an odd

comfort having the events of the last few months reduced to a childhood misdemeanour. But he wasn't a child, and the consequences weren't a scraped boat or broken ornament but real lives. Real hearts. Logan took a sip of his beer, needing to fortify himself before launching into an explanation of his relationship with Willow, from the moment he had pulled her back from a car, through his surfing accident, the partial memory return and blurting out her name, and the solution he had come up with to save her job. It was hard to look at his father during this part, although his dad was as granite-faced as ever, just a ticking of his jaw betraying any emotion at all. Laying bare the lack of trust and communication between his father and him was one of the hardest things Logan had ever done, each word an effort.

It was a relief to move on to his trip to London and the bargain they had struck. He brushed over most of the next four months. After all, both men had witnessed much of it. He skipped to the night of the Fourth of July party, less than two weeks ago. It felt like a lifetime. He ended with the letter he had written her and his own trip out of town to allow her the space to leave, and then he sat back, drained. 'Now you know it all.'

'When did you buy the cottage?' his uncle

asked, and Logan stared at him. He'd expected recriminations, anger, not a mild-mannered question.

'The day after she mentioned it. I wanted her to have something safe to go back to. I wanted…' He stumbled over the next words, a little mortified by the sentimentality. 'I wanted her dreams to come true.'

'And why did you ask her to stay?' his father asked.

'Come on, Dad, have you *met* her?'

'This isn't about me. Why did *you* ask her?'

'Because she was happy here. She fit in.' Neither man said anything, but Logan saw them exchange unreadable glances.

'Go on,' Connor said.

'Because she's pretty near perfect. I didn't want to think about an end point.'

'Do you love her?'

If anyone had told Logan that one day he would be sitting having a drink with his father and uncle discussing love, he would have laughed. Just the shared drink alone would have seemed impossible, the thought of talking about love a far-fetched fantasy. And yet here they were.

'I like her.'

'Logan…' his uncle said, and Logan glared at him.

'Of course I love her!' The words burst

from him with an inevitability and rightness he hadn't known, hadn't recognised. He repeated them slowly, quietly. 'Of course I do.' Willow, so solemn and clever, outwardly sober and respectable and yet with that hidden impulsive side, that sweet wit and kind heart. The only woman—the only person—he had ever really opened up to. That instant connection, like he was coming home. Of course he loved her. He just hadn't recognised that was what this all-encompassing feeling was.

'And did you tell her?'

How could he have when he hadn't known himself until this moment? Besides… 'It wouldn't be fair. It's not part of our agreement.'

'So you bought her a cottage and sent her home and came to me to fall on your sword?' His father sat back and raised an eyebrow. 'Very noble.'

Logan felt his jaw lock into place. 'After everything else, I'm not going to burden her with this.'

'Why would it be a burden?' He hadn't even noticed Sofia join them until she spoke, reaching out to take his hand. He squeezed her fingers, grateful for her presence.

'I don't want to put her under any pressure, any obligation.'

'Logan, darling,' Sofia said, 'have you considered that she might love you too?'

Had he *what*? 'No.'

'Why not?' his father of all people asked.

Logan picked up his drink and realised his hands were trembling, and he carefully set it down. He spent his life avoiding emotion, avoiding conflict, using sport and humour and adrenaline to keep it at bay, but now he was surrounded on all sides, unable to escape the questions, the revelations, the feelings. 'You know why.'

'What on earth do you mean?' his father asked.

'Because you don't love me,' Logan said slowly and deliberately, trying to keep any emotion out of his voice. 'I'm a disappointment, aren't I, Dad? The only thing I have ever done you approved of was marrying Willow, and even that wasn't real. Sometimes I think my mother couldn't have loved me either. Otherwise she would have stayed. She wouldn't have left me alone with you.' As soon as the words were out, he wanted to recall them. How could he have been so weak? Made himself so vulnerable? 'It's okay.' He managed to summon that old insouciant smile, the one that had served him well over the years. 'I'm used to it. But I won't put Willow through having to let me down. It's not fair.'

'Oh, Logan,' Sofia whispered, her fingers tightening around his. 'My poor boy.'

'Of course your mother loved you. She adored you. You were everything to her.' His father sounded abrupt, annoyed, but was that a shimmer of tears in his eyes? Surely not. It must be a trick of the light.

'You never talk about her,' Logan said.

'Because it hurts. Because I am consumed by guilt, still to this day. You asked why I never married again, Logan. How could I when my harsh words, my inability to compromise, led to such a tragedy? When I see myself repeating the same mistakes with my son as I did with my wife? You are so like your mother, Logan, it hurts me to this day. It doesn't mean I'm not proud of you, that I don't love you. I just don't know how to show it. But if I can offer you any advice, it's this. Don't be as proud as I was. Don't let fear stop you. If you love her, tell her so. Be happy, Logan. That's all I can ask. Don't live the rest of your life with regret. It's a lonely way to be.'

'Your mother loved you so much,' Sofia

told him, her hand still in his. 'And she would tell you to listen to your father. She would tell you that love is the greatest adventure of all, with the biggest highs and, yes, the biggest lows, but it's an adventure worth embarking on. Go and find your wife, Logan. Tell her how you feel.'

It was all too much. Twenty-five years' worth of tears and abandonment and hurt were threatening to break through. Logan was almost shaking with the pain of keeping them confined. All he wanted, all he needed, was Willow. 'What if it's too late?'

'There's only one way to find out,' his father said. 'And we are all right behind you.'

CHAPTER THIRTEEN

WILLOW WOKE UP to the disorientation of a strange hotel room, the unnatural darkness of blackout blinds, and the whir of the air conditioning. She blinked, the jet lag and the myriad emotions that had consumed her over the last few weeks rushing back to her in a relentless wave. And now here she was, back in Vegas where it had all begun.

It was the last place she wanted to be. Over the last week she had see-sawed between whether to pick her life back up in London or return to Romney to confront Logan, to be honest with him and tell him how she felt. Skye, as she had expected, had urged her to go back, but then, her sister was an incurable romantic. It didn't help that Logan hadn't yet returned to HartCo, taking a brief leave of absence to finalise the Lona recruitment process. If she could just see him even through a computer screen, she might have an idea of whether returning was a good idea. But although she had been prepared to return to the US, Vegas had not entered into her calculations.

But her feelings didn't matter. She had promised Logan's father during that last excruciating interview where she had told him how Logan had tried to protect her, told him what a clever, compassionate, wonderful son he had, that if he allowed her to stay at HartCo, whether in her old or new role, she would make sure he didn't regret it. If he wanted her at a meeting in Vegas, then this is where she would be, her own discomfort pushed to one side.

So here she was, ready to meet with the board of a media start-up Logan's dad was interested in investing in. She was here to look over the accounts, yes, but there were plenty of people who could do that. She also had to launch a charm offensive, and that was new. Willow walked over to the window and looked down at the city spread before her. The city where it had all began. It all felt so daunting alone, but she knew with Logan by her side it would have been an adventure. Life had been an adventure.

And she had loved every minute of it.

It still could be, if she was brave enough to reach out for it.

She had to be brave enough. She wouldn't

go home after her meeting. She would return to Boston. She would tell him she loved him, clearly, spelled out in three short words. What he did with that information was up to him. But if she didn't tell him, how could she ever move on? He deserved to know, and she deserved to be heard.

It was a relief to have made a decision, and doing so freed her. The last time she had been in the city, she had spent her days in the hotel where the conference was being held, even during her free time, apart from that one last day. Today she was not making the same mistake. Willow showered and dressed before swallowing some breakfast, consuming more coffee, grabbing a bag and her sunglasses and heading out.

The heat was like a solid wall of hot air, a stark contrast to the chill of the air conditioning, forcing Willow to take it slowly as she finally strolled along the famous Strip, following the path as it climbed up and away from the street and through some of the iconic hotel complexes, all trying to lure her in with their blend of food, entertainment, shops, luxury and gambling. She stopped off at an aquarium for a half hour and was tempted into one of the rooftop spa areas for an outdoor swim and massage, before treating herself to a cocktail with lunch. Afterwards she explored some of the more famous hotel complexes, watching couples sail in gondolas and enjoying the spectacular Bellagio fountain show. It wasn't an unpleasant day, especially after the long plane journey the day before, but she was aware of a strange sense of loneliness unusual for her. She had always been so comfortable with her own company before. Maybe it was being here, where she and Logan had first met. She kept her gaze averted from any wedding chapels, but she couldn't avoid seeing newlyweds at every turn. It was a relief to return to her luxurious suite to get ready for the first meeting with the start-up.

It was with no small measure of shyness that she left the sanctuary of her suite and headed for the bar. At least she had a reserved table so she wouldn't have the awkwardness of trying to figure out who she was meeting. And she had the confidence of knowing she looked her best in a cream cocktail dress shot through with matt gold thread, the full skirt falling to just above her knees, the sleeveless bodice closely fitted. She'd pinned her hair up in an approximation of the style she'd worn for the Fourth of July party and made an effort with her make-up so her eyes were smoky, her lips raspberry red. A matt gold wrap, matching strappy sandals and a clutch bag, completed the look. She wasn't Willow Jones, more comfortable with numbers than people. She was a representative of the Hartwell family.

Willow was aware of admiring looks as she left the lift and made her way across the lobby to the special elevator that served the exclusive rooftop cocktail bar where she was due to meet her guests. Part of her expected to be challenged, but she was bowed through by the bellboy, and the glass lift was soon making its dizzying way up to the very top of the building. All too soon she was stepping out into the greenery of the rooftop garden and cocktail bar, where she was greeted and shown to her table, a discreet shielded corner with breathtaking views, and handed the menu. Willow might have been living with a self-made millionaire and heir to a much larger fortune for the last few months, but their meals out had been as likely to be at a food court or Logan's uncle's Inn as a fancy restaurant, and the prices took her breath away.

A couple of minutes passed with no sign of her guests, but as she pulled her phone out of her bag to check to see if she had any messages, a shadow fell over the table, and a voice she knew all too well asked: 'Is this seat taken?'

* * *

She looked beautiful. Of course she did. Willow always looked beautiful, but tonight she was especially so, sophisticated and elegant, mistress of her surroundings. Her eyes widened with shock as he approached but, Logan was relieved to note, they immediately softened in welcome.

'Logan, what are you doing here? Are you coming to this meeting too?'

'The meeting isn't until tomorrow,' he said. 'I got your PA to get you here a day early. I wanted to talk.'

Some of the warmth melted away as she stiffened almost imperceptibly. 'You have my number, Logan. You could have spoken to me at any time, rather than leave me plane tickets to send me home and resort to subterfuge to bring me back.'

'I do, I could, and I know I owe you an apology. More than one.' He stopped and smiled at her. 'You look amazing.'

'Thank you.' She paused, then said slightly grudgingly, 'You look nice too.'

He pulled at his tie. It was too hot for a suit really, even a linen one, but he had wanted to look smart for her.

At that moment, the waitress brought over the bottle of champagne he had ordered when he arrived, and neither said anything as the cork was popped and the glasses poured. Logan made no move to take his glass. He had too much to say first.

'Like I say, I owe you several apologies. For going back on my word about the annulment and then dragging you into a deception. For walking away the second I couldn't handle my feelings and sending you away. For deceiving you just now. For not being honest with you over the last few months, but to be fair, I wasn't being honest with myself either.'

'I haven't been entirely honest with you either,' Willow said, toying with her napkin. 'That night on the beach, there were things I should have told you, things I could have said in the week we spent together afterwards, but I was afraid, Logan. I had my future all planned out, and then you came along, and everything I thought I wanted changed. It took me a long time to recognise that, and then when I did, I just walked away rather than fight for it, fight for us.'

That *us* emboldened Logan more than anything else could have done. 'I didn't think I was capable of loving or being loved,' he said quickly before he could change his mind. 'I used charm and humour and my lifestyle to avoid any commitment, anything serious...'

'That's not entirely true. You showed commitment to your employees. You were serious about your business. The clues were always there, Logan.'

'Part of me thought my dad was right. He was my father, Willow. If he didn't love me, then what did that make me? I know my mother's death was an accident, but she went without saying goodbye. I called after her, but she didn't turn back.'

Her eyes were huge, shimmering with tears. 'Oh, Logan.'

'So you see, I didn't realise I'd fallen in love with you. I didn't recognise it. I just knew I wanted you with me always. That I was a better man when you were with me. That I enjoyed your company above all else. That I wanted to make you happy.'

'You bought me my house.'

'Do you like it?'

'It's perfect apart from one thing. It's a little lonely.'

Logan took a deep breath. 'I love you, Willow Jones. I love your brains and your to-do lists. I love the moments when you forget about being a sensible member of society and let go. I love your bravery and compassion. I love you, and whatever happens next, I will never regret that. I am a better man because of knowing you, loving you.' It was all he had, but it didn't seem enough. 'I love you,' he repeated.

Willow wiped a finger under her eyes. 'Damn eye make-up.' She sniffed. 'If you make me cry, I'll look like a panda. I love you too, Logan. I think I did the moment you put those chips in my hand and dared me to step out of my comfort zone, and I have loved you more every day since.'

He reached across the table and she took his hand, their fingers enclosing around each other. 'You're still wearing it.' He caressed the silver ring he had bought her at the chapel, the ring she had been wearing since returning to the States with him, not allowing him to replace it. *They'll assume it's platinum*, she had said, and as usual, she had been right.

'I haven't taken it off.'

Logan picked up his glass and held it out to her. 'Then, Willow Jones, will you stay with me as my wife? Not for a year or until it's no longer easy, but forever?'

She touched her glass to his, her smile tremulous, eyes still swimming with tears. 'Oh, Logan. Of course I will.'

Willow wanted nothing more than to grab the champagne and take Logan back to her hotel suite, but after she had finished the glass, he asked for the bottle to be sent to their room and pulled Willow to her feet. 'There's something I want you to see,' he said.

She turned to him, sliding her hand to his nape, pulling him close as she kissed him softly. 'I already went to the aquarium.'

'It's not the aquarium.'

'I'm not in the mood for gambling, even if I do feel like the luckiest girl in the world tonight.'

'Not a casino. Come on.'

They took the glass elevator back down to the ground floor, hand in hand, Willow unable to believe that this was happening, that Logan was here with her. Logan held on to her tightly as they exited the lift, then guided her through the back of the hotel to the taxi drop-off spot where a car was waiting.

'The Grand Canyon for a midnight picnic?' she guessed.

'Sounds fun, but not today.'

She continued to make increasingly wild suggestions as the car took them a short distance through the busy neon-lit streets until it stopped beside a familiar white wooden building with a small tower and a big sign proclaiming Walk-in Weddings Available Here. Willow didn't say a word as Logan stepped out of the car and came round to her door, opened it and helped her out. He kept hold of her hand as he sank to one knee, and for the third time in her life, she heard him utter the words: 'Willow Jones, would you do me the honour of being my wife?'

'Logan, what on earth? You don't have to do this,' she protested.

'The first time I asked you was for one night, the second for one year. This time I am asking you not because it feels like fun, or because it serves a purpose, but because I love you. Willow, I'm not exaggerating when I say you make me the happiest of men, happier than I ever thought I could be, than I deserved to be. Will you marry me?'

'Yes. Of course I will.' She pulled him up and kissed him. 'Any time.'

He reached into his jacket pocket and pulled out a small square box. 'This was my mother's. If you don't like it, we can have it restyled, but my father thought it would be a fitting gesture.'

'Your father? That was very thoughtful.' And unexpected. A lot had clearly happened while she had been away. Logan just nodded as he opened the box to show her a beautiful antique ring, a square-cut sapphire surrounded by an oval of diamonds.

'It's art deco. My mother loved vintage jewellery, antiques. She liked things that had already lived, she always said. My father bought this for her because the sapphire made him think of the ocean, and the ocean made him think of her. Looks like he does have a romantic bone in his body after all.'

'I love it. I really do.' She held her breath as he eased the wedding ring off her finger and slid the engagement one on. 'It fits.'

To her surprise, the driver handed her a bouquet of flowers, and as she turned to thank him, Logan dropped a quick kiss onto her cheek, pocketing her wedding ring as he did so. 'I'm heading in. See you in there.'

'Logan!' Willow stood on the kerb, holding the bouquet, and watched him jog into the chapel. She'd expected they would walk in there together like they had last time for the brief ceremony, not that she would be entering alone. It was all very romantic, of course, but she had barely had a chance to get her head around the realisation that Logan was here, that he loved her, let alone this surprise ceremony.

If they were going to renew their vows, it would just be nice if her family were here. But he had gone to so much effort, she couldn't ask to postpone.

At that moment, a man exited the chapel, and for one second she thought it was Logan again, until she blinked and realised it was someone completely different. 'Dad? What are you doing here? You look so smart,' she added. It wasn't often that he wore a suit.

'I've come to give you away,' her father said gruffly. 'Oh, Willow, you look so beautiful.'

In a daze she kissed his cheek. 'I can't believe it. I was just wishing you were here, and then you appeared. Mia! Harper!' Her nieces ran up to her, both in pretty white dresses and clutching matching bouquets to hers. 'When did you get here?'

'Yesterday! Mummy said it was a surprise. Are you very surprised, Aunty Willow?'

'More than I have ever been in my life,' she assured them, as they danced ahead of her to the chapel door.

'Are you sure?' her dad asked as they reached the foyer and Willow squeezed his arm. 'This Logan, is he the right man for you?'

'He is, Dad, and I really am sure. To have you all here is just perfect.'

The music started, and Mia and Harper, who had obviously been practising, made their way down the short aisle. On one side, Willow saw her mother in a huge hat sat next to her brother and sisters, Skye looking very smug as she leaned into Jack. How long had her sister been helping Logan arrange this? She smiled her thanks as Skye blew her a kiss.

On the other side, Connor and Sofia sat with Logan's father, Nate propped on his crutches at the front next to Logan.

And then she was standing by the altar, her hands entwined with Logan's, their eyes fastened on each other as they repeated the words they had first said several months before, but this time with love and meaning and with their families to witness and bless them.

Willow's heart was full. She had stepped out of her comfort zone and gambled her happiness and her heart on this man who was looking at her as if no one else existed in the world. That gamble had paid off in ways she had never expected or dreamed of. She knew that life with Logan might not fit neatly into a to-do list, but it would never be dull—and that he would give her the security she needed in all the ways it mattered most. And in return she would give him all the love he had thought he wasn't worthy of. She had already given him her heart.

'You may kiss the bride,' the bewigged, drawling Elvis impersonator finally concluded, and Willow smiled up into Logan's dark blue eyes.

'I love you,' she whispered. 'Thank you for making me so very happy.'

'I love you too,' he said, kissing her amidst whoops and cheers from their families. 'And

I promise you, here and now, to always do my best to make you happy.'

'Me too,' she vowed, and as she kissed him again, she knew that this final promise was the most important of all. 'Me too.'

* * * * *

If you enjoyed this story, check out these other great reads from Jessica Gilmore

Christmas with His Ballerina
The Princess and the Single Dad
Cinderella and the Vicomte
Christmas with His Cinderella

All available now!